SCISSORS

STÉPHANE MICHAKA

SCISSORS

Stéphane Michaka was born in Paris in 1974. He studied at Cambridge University and taught French in South Africa before embarking on a writing career. He has written theater pieces, children's books, television scripts, and radio plays. *Scissors* is his third novel.

s c i s | s o r s

A NOVEL

STÉPHANE MICHAKA

Translated from the French by John Cullen

ANCHOR BOOKS
A Division of Random House LLC
New York

FIRST ANCHOR BOOKS EDITION, MAY 2014

The Library of Congress has cataloged the Nan A. Talese/Doubleday
edition as follows:
Michaka, Stéphane.
[Ciseaux. English]
Scissors : a novel / Stéphane Michaka ; translated from the French
by John Cullen. — First American Edition.
pages cm.
Includes bibliographical references.
1. Carver, Raymond, 1938–1988—Friends and associates—Fiction.
2. Biographical fiction. I. Cullen, John, translator. II. Title.
PQ2713.I235C5713 2013
843'.92—dc23 2012046949

Anchor Trade Paperback ISBN: 978-0-345-80558-4
eBook ISBN: 978-0-385-53751-3

Book design by Maria Carella

www.anchorbooks.com

150153857

For Lilas

AUTHOR'S NOTE

Scissors is a work of fiction. Although I have used some publicly known facts from Raymond Carver's life and from his relationship with his editor, Gordon Lish, the characters in this novel are loosely based, rather than closely modeled, on real-life figures. My characters' words, as well as the four short stories included in *Scissors,* are all my invention. For nonfictional surveys of Raymond Carver's life and work, which will no doubt continue to inspire readers and writers alike, the reader is directed to the selected bibliography at the end of this volume.

SCISSORS

RAYMOND

What comes over us is pretty scary. It takes hold without warning. Even when nothing's going on, it's there. It's waiting. A delayed explosion, that's it, that's precisely what it is: a time bomb.

The alcoholic's internal clock is the thing we've all come here to get rid of.

Paula and Cathy, the directors of this center, are unfailingly patient. They need patience with guys like us. And they have a sense of humor too—who could do without one in their line of work? Whenever somebody starts to shake, a sure sign of an imminent attack, Paula or Cathy comes over and says, "We must pull our tongue in, we mustn't let it hang out of our mouth." And then you find that one or the other of them, or the big fat guy when he's on duty, has their thumbs between your teeth. Some people bite themselves bloody.

I checked in yesterday. It's not the first time I've come here, but I'd like it to be the best time. The last time.

Two days ago, I broke a bottle on Marianne's head.

In the fifteen years we've been married, that's never happened before. Marianne provoked me, of course. I'll spare you the details. I love Marianne and as she often tells me, she couldn't live without me. Maybe the bottle was on account of that.

I'm going to give you the details after all. We had a housewarming party at our new place in town. Alcohol was flowing like a mighty river, and Marianne started flirting with one of my colleagues. A history professor, I think. "Hey," I said to my wife. "Am I seeing right? Are you letting him check out your tits?" I should have whacked the guy, but Marianne was the one who got it. The bottle broke against her skull. She raised herself off the floor and left the house. She was found staggering down the street. The doctors told me an artery was cut and she'd lost half her blood.

Half her blood gone and still walking: that's Marianne.

The most embarrassing thing is I don't remember hitting her. Some of our friends told me about it afterward. "I don't remember anything," I said. "Not a thing." They looked at me as though I'd killed someone.

I felt so bad I packed my bag and left.

I landed here.

*

I know I have to call Marianne and apologize. For that and for all the rest. But whenever I go to the telephone, there's a long line of guys waiting to do a whole lot of apologizing to a whole lot of people. Just listening to them makes your head spin. You'd think the worst criminals on the planet had somehow wound up here. Some of them manage to pull through. They start over from scratch. After they get past withdrawal, I mean. You see, the problem's in your body. It's your system that's dependent. And then one fine day it isn't anymore, but that takes awhile.

*

I don't know how long I'm going to stay here, but this will be the last time, I think. It's a great place as long as you don't have an urgent phone call to make. Paula and Cathy bought the land from a retired farmer. There's a dilapidated farmhouse at the end of the road. Its doors and windows are boarded up. Right in front of it, there's a chestnut tree that drops leaves all year round. One day it's going to fall on the farmhouse. Farther on there's the paved road, and about a mile and a half away there's alcohol for sale. We're not allowed to venture that far. I found a little stream near the fence. A thin thread of water with pebbles on either side.

I kneel down and think about Marianne. About what I'd like to tell her. Some sad things, consoling things, and some other things, too.

Maybe she never wants to see me again.

*

People are always assuring us we don't live in a world of certainties. We're told there's nothing certain but love, so long as it lasts; the family, so long as it stays together; and friends, when they're passing through. Which is the same as saying that none of all that is any surer than anything else. And so? Does that mean we have to do without certainties? Can you hold out for very long without one or two stones in your hand?

Marianne and I live near a river. Our children are grown up now. Well, almost grown up. They don't go down to the river with us anymore to catch trout or skip stones. I try to guard against it, but every time I throw a stone, I feel a twinge of fear. A superstition. There's one less stone in my hand, and I'm going to have to make do. To live without the smallest certainty. In the catastrophe of complete uncertainty.

I don't think my stories have ever been about anything else.

My name is Raymond. I'm a writer. That is, I hope to become one.

DOUGLAS

All my days are alike. That's something I wanted. *A victory, you can say.*

I look out the window. *You can't say window.* It's a glass panel, a transparent solid overlooking the city. A cleaning person washes it down with soapy water three times a week (the panel pivots around) and then goes over it with a rubber broom. I'm rarely in the room when she does that. At the time when she comes, I'm generally dictating a letter to Sibyll or downstairs having lunch somewhere near the magazine's offices. There are so many restaurants I haven't come close to trying them all. Here's the advantage of working in the publishing district: The good tables are always opening and closing. Like publishers. A series of openings, failures, and reopenings. *There are no disasters, just different ways of trying your luck.* One of my mottoes. I have heaps of mottoes.

When the worker assigned to window cleaning finishes on this floor, she goes on to the next. I've never asked her whether she moves her operation one floor up or one floor down. There are twenty floors in this building. Window cleaning on that scale requires a method. Or maybe a dozen people like her. I don't know her name. The girl with the rubber broom. You could make a novel out of that. Sometimes I get the itch to do that sort of thing. But I restrain myself. My imagination is concise. My work is reduction. I edit short stories, epics in miniature.

The girl has a rubber broom, and ten pages on, all you'll know about her life is that she goes down one floor after another, cleaning windows. Or maybe up. I like to leave things blurry.

*

It's time. At a certain point in the day, depending on the weather, the light comes in from the west. It caresses the side of the building, but only from the floor below on up. It rubs its muzzle against the glass—*it's an image, don't over-use it*, I tell my students. *An image is a beauty mark; when it's close to another one, it becomes a wart.* The light rounds its back against my panes and *shhh—an example of onomatopoeia; two are allowed, but they must be comic in intent.* You can see it at this very moment: the prism of colors. An effect that requires no fewer than sixty-six colored panes. This rose window cost me an arm and a leg. It never fails to thrill me.

People sometimes ask me, "Suppose you get fired? If they fire you from the magazine, what will they do about your stained-glass window?"

If they fire me, what will they do about their magazine? It's entirely dependent on the stories I buy and publish. The voice you hear inside. Readers come to listen to that voice.

I'm not God. Who said I thought I was God? I have enemies everywhere in the publishing business. In rival houses, at other magazines. Enemies spreading like a case of psoriasis I purposely encourage. I love the constant eruption of envy around me.

Don't think for a minute this stained-glass window can't be removed. Like every one of us here below.

What else? Nothing for the moment. For the moment, this day is like the others, and the girl with the rubber broom has already taken up too much of my attention.

Oh, I almost forgot: My name is Douglas. People in the business call me "Scissors."

RAYMOND

That was a goose, right? I thought I heard a goose.

Geese have a way of squawking that imposes a brief period of silence. Then everything starts chirping and buzzing again, just like before.

Those brusque interruptions remind me of the first years of my marriage. I was young, I needed air, so did Marianne, but I didn't let her have any.

We were kids, with two children we'd had too soon. What

do you do when the road behind you closes and you can't back up anymore? I wrote a story about that: "Who Needs Air?"

I'd like to take it up again, revise it, improve it. This morning Paula asked me, "What do you love most in life? What is it you want to preserve at all costs?"

I didn't say, "My wife." I didn't say, "Marianne and the children."

I said, "My stories."

Good God, I said my stories.

Who Needs Air?

Ambulance sirens, that's what I bring home with me from my nights on duty.

From midnight to eight in the morning, the sirens follow one another, or sometimes blend together, on the two-lane road that circles the hospital. I can hear them from my night-watchman's box, first far, then close, and finally not at all, when the lights are still on but the sound is off and the ambulances park in the back, unburdened of an injured person or a corpse.

At the moment, my thoughts go no farther than that. To me, emergencies are distant sounds I hear from inside a glass cage.

But when the night's over and I sit down to write, the sirens return and haunt me. They get mixed up with other sirens, with specific catastrophes engraved in my memory.

Like the time in the sawmill where my father worked, the Big Gully sawmill. I went there after school one day to learn something about the work, and I saw a man, Frank Dubont, whose arms no longer ended in hands. The foreman said Frank was drunk and had leaned over the saw so it would carry him away. But the saw had taken only his hands. I turned to my father. I figured he was going to tell me not to stay. His eyelids were red and his lips were trembling. I averted my eyes. The teeth of the saw were intact and gleaming with blood. As I was leaving on my bicycle, I passed the ambulance coming in.

Another siren comes back to me from one Christmas

when the snow never stopped coming down. The scene was our neighbors' house. They were Carole and Ben Weber, and they'd been separated for a month. Now Ben was living in a mobile home owned by his mistress, Betty Pradinas. Carole's best friend up until a month ago. I don't know what Ben could have been thinking, but he showed up at the house to wish Carole a merry Christmas. Maybe she lured him with some tasty little dishes (Betty knows how to do lots of things, but cooking isn't one of them). In any case, Ben got served. Three bullets from a .22. Who would have thought Carole Weber kept a rifle in her vegetable garden? A rifle and some Ajax for killing slugs. Ben didn't die, he was just perforated. By love, of course, it was love that perforated him. Betty's mobile home wasn't seen again.

A siren never far from my mind: the one in the ambulance taking Marion to the hospital. It's her second pregnancy, and there are complications. I'm at her side. While I hold her hand—her fingers are too weak to squeeze mine—I start thinking, *So what if...?* If she lost the baby, that might not be a tragedy. A doctor's leaning over her. With a quick look, he checks on how I'm holding up. Why on earth am I making this face? Playing the anxious guy? The truth is I'm saying to myself, *It might not be a tragedy.* The doctor concentrates on my wife. I keep on thinking, *So what if...?* I'm twenty years old. Marion's eighteen. She got pregnant again three months after our first baby. By the time she realized what was up, it was too late.

With the siren drilling my ears, I have the impression that Marion and I are driving right into a wall.

My son is born the next day. Theo.

Marion's better. She turns her face to me, her drawn features, her pale smile. I love her so much I could go nuts from it. And I don't hear the siren anymore.

I should be at my typewriter, working. But as so often, I'm a truant. I don't go home when my night duty's over. Not right away. I take the exit ramp, park my car, and wait. While my limbs grow numb and grayish condensation fogs the windshield, I wait for the grocery store to open. So I can get, in exchange for a five-dollar bill and a grunt that means good morning, the bottle of whiskey I crave.

The truth is I really like to drink. I like the taste of liquor. Everything would be a lot simpler if I didn't like it so much.

It warms me up very quickly. It's an old acquaintance, a friend waiting patiently on the doorstep. Why leave him outside? He joins me and makes me warm. There in the car, when the bottle rolls at my feet and strikes the other bottles, I can no longer feel my legs, the cold, or remorse.

On the way home, in the comfort zone where the sirens fade away, nothing has any consequences. It's the hour when my actions are just a rough draft. I could delete a whole day's worth. I forget that I'll flop down on the sofa as soon as I get inside and fall into a sleep that will delete nothing but rather insert, insert deeper in me remorse for getting drunk.

I forget that I want to be a writer.

It's a Monday in November. Monday is laundry day. I'm the one who takes care of the laundry. Dead leaves are piling up on the windowsills. The leaves block the rain gutters. I have to take care of that too.

In the evenings, when Marion comes home, the kids are already in bed. As for whether or not they're asleep, I don't know. That's another story.

"You ought to go and check on them," Marion says, taking out the silverware.

"It's ten o'clock. My shift's over, right?"

She flings the knives down on the kitchen table.

"Your shift? You worked a shift? Then why isn't the laundry done? Why has nothing been ironed?"

"I didn't have time."

She moves a knife and looks daggers at me, as if I'm the one throwing the cutlery around.

"I was at the Laundromat. I spent the whole afternoon there."

"Hard to tell," Marion says.

"I was at the Laundromat, and something happened."

"Please, Robin, no stories. I'm not in the mood to—"

"Just listen. Listen to what happened in the Laundromat."

She sits down, opens a beer, and pours it into a glass. I can't get over it. I thought I drank them all. Does she have a secret compartment in the fridge?

I suppress a trembling fit and the urge to dismantle the fridge.

"You can tell me your story while I drink," Marion says.

I can see she's dying to hear it. My wife loves listening to my stories. She likes inventing them too, but she doesn't make it her job. Marion pays the rent and the household expenses. That's the way the roles have been assigned. She's challenging me to tell the story. I don't want to disappoint her.

"So I'm in the Laundromat. The place is packed. Mothers with children who should be in school. Why aren't they in school? I don't know if you're aware of this, but not all the children in our neighborhood go to school. They're playing hooky, I suppose. Are you listening to me?"

"I'm listening to you, Robin."

"And those are the kids Sophie and Theo play hide-and-seek with."

"What could you possibly know about that?"

She puts down her glass so hard it shakes the table.

"Well, hide-and-seek or some other game."

"You have no proof they're playing hooky."

"In any case, lots of kids. There's a tremendous racket in the Laundromat. The machines spin and spin without stopping, or rather when one *does* stop, a sturdy matron doing her entire family's winter underwear is right there to fill it up. And then she restarts the machine, the racket gets louder again, and I'm obliged to wait, to endure, trapped on a bench with three bags of dirty clothes: one Sophie's and Theo's, one yours, and one mine, like it's been ever since we started separating the laundry. Incidentally, why do we separate it?"

"You have more white, that's all. You have more white than I do."

"Anyway, I'm there with my bags, wondering how long

I'm going to have to hang around. I look at my watch. The children get out of school in an hour. I'm not talking about the children who are running around in the Laundromat. I'm talking about our children, who go to school."

She lights a cigarette.

"I got that already," she says. "You should cut that. Those last sentences."

She pulls the ashtray closer.

"Those sentences have some importance," I reply. "They're important, and you'll see why later."

I'm on the point of resuming the story when I have the sudden feeling that I'm suffocating. It's a repeat of the feeling that overcame me in the Laundromat.

I'm afraid I'll start shaking. I turn to open a window. I lift it a few inches.

"Who needs air?" Marion says.

I look at her. I realize I've lost the thread.

" 'Those sentences are important,' " she repeats, helping me out. "But wait. I thought I heard Theo."

"It must have come from outside."

We listen. Muffled voices and the TV set in the opposite apartment, where our neighbors turn the thing on and never watch it. A damp smell enters the kitchen. Marion shakes her head. "That's not Theo," she says.

"You want me to go and see?"

"Shouldn't you be getting ready to leave?"

I look at the clock and see myself in the Laundromat again, staring at the hands of the clock on the wall.

"So school's out soon. I'm thinking there's no way—I mean *no way* at all, even if I perform some fabulous feat—

to finish with the wash before I have to go and pick up the kids from school. At that moment, the matron opens two machines. Two opportunities present themselves. I charge over to them, so impulsively I forget the laundry bags. You know that in a Laundromat, in the lawless primitive jungle of a Laundromat, no discussion is possible. There's no language, no way to assert yourself, other than dumping a massive load of laundry into the machine as it's being cleared. And I forget the bags. I forget and pull up flabbergasted in front of the matron. 'Thanks,' she says. 'I don't need any help.' She refills the machines, closes the doors, and punches in the programs. I stand there like an idiot, with my three bags at the other end of the Laundromat. I head back to the bench. Someone's taken my place."

"Close the window, Robin."

"It's stifling in here."

"Close the window, the kids are going to catch colds."

She stubs out her cigarette. While she's lighting up another one—the ashtray is overflowing, how can she have any left?—I pivot and lift the window higher.

"I'm stifling, me!"

When I turn around, there's no anger on her face. She comes close to me. Cigarette in hand, she puts her arms around me and lays her forehead against my chest.

I hear the TV, the muffled voices, and a crying child.

"Theo," I murmur.

She raises her head. We freeze and listen.

I think about the cartons of cigarettes she keeps with her stockings and the secret compartment in the fridge.

Marion leaves the kitchen. I start to shake. I feel an irresistible desire to search the fridge.

She comes back and says, "It wasn't Theo."

Marion sits down again. I resume my story. The window's down, but it's still cold.

I put some water on to boil and tell her the whole story.

I tell her what I felt in the Laundromat. Running from one chore to another, from one child to the other, from Theo to Sophie and from Sophie to Theo. How can I write? I don't mean a novel, I've given up any hope of that, but at least some short stories, stories that don't take long to put together. I haven't had even enough time to write stories for the last five years. We used to talk about doing things, we said we had to keep moving. We had some ambitions and all sorts of dreams. Now we have three loans to repay, we don't have enough money for the heating bill, and the washing machine's been repossessed. No magazine wants to publish my stories. Nothing's moving, I'm not writing anymore, I'm bound hand and foot. And you know what? Those kids in the Laundromat, they're there because their parents don't have the time to pick them up after school. And I can't do the wash because I have to go get my kids . . . Lots of people are better organized than we are. "So you see," I tell her, "those sentences had some importance."

The kettle starts whistling. Marion looks at me incredulously.

"How dare you say that? How do you dare tell me all that? You want me to describe my day to you? Is this a contest? The parent with the biggest ball and chain and the worst day wins the prize? Because I'm not so sure it would be you. I don't think it would even be a tie."

She's talking over the whistling kettle. She moves it without burning herself. How does she do that without burning herself? Sometimes I think my wife's fireproof.

"You have two jobs. The hospital and the library. You're a night watchman at the hospital and three afternoons a week you're a librarian." (She counts on her fingers. I look at her hand and see it stroking my face.) "I, on the other hand, am a waitress. I wait tables at the university, at the Athletic Club. Every time I put my apron on, I tell myself I'm the athlete, I'm the one who's athletic. An athlete in the morning and an athlete in the afternoon. In the afternoon, I stop at the parent institute and pick up my kits. I pick up my kits and begin to go door-to-door. Just describing the kit to the customer and explaining how it works takes a good twenty minutes. 'No, it's not a first-aid kit, it's a kit for educating your children.' I smile from ear to ear and keep some jokes in reserve—jokes are part of the job. Try selling a kit without a smile, just try it and see. You sell the kit and the smile sells you. That's what I tell myself. And when I explain that to the boss, he talks about giving me a promotion. You could be the regional supervisor, he tells me. Would you like to be the regional supervisor? I started the job three weeks ago and he's talking about promoting me. Pretty athletic, huh? After I make my rounds, I stop off at Winnie's. She lets me use the restroom without ordering anything at the bar. It's a deodorant-stick stop, the one I make at Winnie's, because I can't go on to my next job, flogging programs at the movie theater, if my armpits stink. And while I'm shaking the stick, I look in the mirror and say to myself, 'How am I going to supervise the region if I have to be home by eight o'clock to put the children to bed? How? I'm asking you.' And I don't know why I say that, because I'm not working three jobs just so we can pay the rent and buy clothes for Theo and Sophie and get a new lawn mower—"

"The lawn mower's broken?"

"We don't have a lawn mower, you jackass. You haven't noticed that the grass on the lawn comes up to your knees?" When she adds that last question, she throws her hands in the air. (I love it when she throws her hands in the air.) "What I'm saying is those three jobs aren't just so we can afford to buy stuff. They're supposed to pay for my college too."

I heave a sigh. Marion wants to go far, and nobody better stop her. But we have two children, no diplomas, and debts up to our necks. We're broke, and I don't want to give up writing.

She empties the ashtray and says, "You just ought to stop drinking, Robin."

I blink. "It's under control," I say.

"Under control? You've got your alcohol intake under control? You must be joking!"

While she's getting out another cigarette, I slam my fist on the table. Nobody's impressed. It just hurts my fingers.

And she goes backward, she rewinds her monologue. "Three jobs I can't stand. I feed my family and put some money into my college fund." (She can't find any matches.

For a change, she's run out of something.) "I'm an all-around athlete."

I make a mental note of the alliteration.

"God damn it! Shit!" She bends over the stove and lights her cigarette from the gas burner. She inhales the smoke. She says, "I got a scholarship."

I stay quiet. She goes on: "They're giving me money to continue my studies. I'm going to sign up for either prelaw or literature. I should pick law, right? Baldaccini suggests law."

"Who's that?"

"My adviser. Dr. Balda—"

"I've never seen him."

I pronounce "Baldaccini" a bunch of times, grimacing conspicuously.

"You must have seen him in the library. He's got a beard."

"They all have beards. I'm going to be late," I say, looking at the clock.

I have pins and needles in my legs. Marion strokes the back of her neck. It's a thing she does before making love.

She breaks off the stroking and points to the room where I write. "About the study," she says.

I knew she was going to talk to me about that.

"It's my study."

"We should think about what we're going to do with it."

"It's a protected area. A minefield."

"I know, but you're not writing anything at the moment."

"Have you been searching my study? Who told you I wasn't writing?"

"You did. You're the one who told me. You just said it. We need that room—"

"*You* need that room. For Baldaccini," I add, not completely sure what this is leading to.

"Fuck you, Robin! We need that room for Sophie and Theo. They aren't sleeping well sharing one bed."

"Then we put in another bed!"

"There's not enough room. Not enough room," she repeats. Then she starts to cry.

I walk toward the door. Marion scurries behind me.

"I've always supported you," she gasps out. "I support your writing, your ambitions. We have to help each other."

"Marion . . ."

I don't know where this is leading. I don't have the least idea. I say, "I have to go."

"They want my response about the scholarship. They expect it tomorrow."

She says that, and she's not crying anymore.

There's a silence. When it's over, I come out with, "So, Sophie and Theo—you're going to put them away in a drawer?"

She bursts into sobs, as if I've broken a bottle on her head.

I leave the kitchen. I slam the front door and go down the walkway.

Outside at last.

What am I going to do with my life?

I head for the car. Some children begin to cry. I don't know if they're ours. I hear a siren and the highway sound in the distance like a great inrush of air.

At the moment when I open the car door, I realize I've

left my keys on the kitchen table. I'm going to have to ring the doorbell and wait for Marion to come to the front door. I'm going to have to go back inside.

I hear a rustling noise. I'm standing in a pile of leaves so deep I can't see my shoes. I think about the secret compartment in the fridge. About all the compartments in all the fridges in the neighborhood. Everybody should have one, I say to myself. A secret place, there or somewhere else.

"You just ought to stop drinking," Marion says as she opens the door.

I close my fingers on the keys she hands me. They're still warm from contact with her palm.

And I start shaking.

DOUGLAS

Of course it's a favor. You think I have nothing to do but entertain all the girl students in the country? Little featherheads with *A Room of One's Own* in one hand and *Cosmopolitan* in the other. And I'm supposed to speak to them and expose my views on fiction? Give me a break. I'll be glad to expose my views, but not on fiction.

You don't want to sit any closer? You prefer the sofa? Fine.

Where was I? Ah yes, fiction. I focus on the real, it's all I'm interested in. Family, work, humiliation, illness, our attempts to escape all of that, and three little notes whistled in the dark before it swallows us up.

I tell my students—I run a writing workshop twice a week, you should come—I tell them, "Pick the most humiliating thing that ever happened to you, the thing that made you feel really, really low. Then take a piece of paper and tell me the story." They all have the same frozen smile as they remember their first french kiss, the first time they went to bed with somebody . . . I yell, WRITE, GOD DAMN IT! They jump exactly the way you just did and start to scratch themselves. What do you think's going on? Inhibitions, blank-page syndrome? Just the opposite. You should see how they put their shame on display, how they jostle one another for the chance to admit their self-loathing. The novices' confessional. I get thirsty just talking about it.

This is bourbon, would you like some? I keep a flask in my right-hand pocket. I can't afford to make a mistake—the other pocket has skin lotion. For my unending psoriasis. Bourbon on the right, on the left oil for my scales. *Scales*, I love that word. "He loved the word, but not the thing." Do you know who wrote that? I could say that about all existence. But then there's the word, you understand what I mean? A word like *existence* or *scales* or *disaster*. And the words are enough to make me hang on to the things, enough to make me want to love them. Just be sure you give me the right word. Not the one word too many. Too many words give me hives. You see my card—here, take my card, I'm doing you a favor—you can see it says there *Literary Editor* and the name of the magazine. I should replace that with *Literary Rash*. That's what I get from ten short stories out of ten. Sometimes the eleventh one comes along, and I scrutinize it, I rework it. I don't quit until it's readable. Notice I didn't say *publishable*. Publishable? One story out of a hundred. One out of a thousand, if I listened to myself. Except that I have a magazine to get out. I have to accept defeat. *Different ways of trying your luck while you're waiting for someone to come along.*

A voice, do you know what that is? I don't hear many real voices these days. But my ears remain open. The magic wand is there, as ready as ever.

Let's go back to my students. They read their disgraceful efforts aloud. My verdict? Always the same: WHO TOLD YOU TO GET NAKED? I have to shout very loud to get it through their heads. WHO TOLD YOU TO POUR YOUR HEART OUT ONTO MY SHOES? I wipe my feet on your heart like a doormat. Who told you to describe a real humiliation? That's what you did, every one of you.

You think I contradict myself? Very well then, I contradict myself. And at the same time, I've defined fiction: *Reality with a sideways step.* Where's yours? Where's your sideways step? That's what I ask my students. Flee sincerity like the plague, I tell them.

You're staring at my mail. That pile of manuscripts. Do I look at all of them? Of course. Do I read them all? Of course not. The first sentence tells me everything. Which means, it tells me whether or not I must read the next one. And so on, right up to the last word, where the decision still hangs in the balance.

You want a test case, is that it? You're a gambler. A gambler has turned up in my office. So much the better, I like girls who . . . I myself am . . . What an idea, putting so much Scotch tape on this thing. The sender must be the anxious type. Give me that paper knife. There, on the coffee table. Thanks. I want to open this myself. People all over the country submit their work to me. The entire nation sends me its stories: white-collar workers, blue-collar workers, immigrants, sales reps, prisoners—some serving life sentences—and the president's wife. You want me to tell you something? *All our secrets are the same.*

Let's see whose these are . . . ah, it's Raymond. What's

he got to tell me? *"Ambulance sirens, that's what I bring home with me from my nights on duty."* Raymond thinks he's the only hospital night watchman in the country. For pity's sake. But make a note, make a note in that little notebook of yours: *"what I bring home with me from my nights on duty."* That's the kind of sentence I run away from before I get to the period.

Poor Raymond, he brings home sirens.

Believe it or not, when I go home, I still haven't had my fill. I pick up a book of fairy tales and read one to my son. "Ithaca," I say to him, "you're not obliged to believe this bullshit." He nods his head. But just so he can get what he wants, which is for me to keep on reading. He's three years old and he's already manipulating me.

So why exactly have you come? You're writing a memoir. You go to see an editor. And you ask him to define fiction. I'm not God the Father. I'm just the Captain of the Storytellers. That moniker has never caught on, I don't know why. I owe my reputation to my skill with scissors, the talent I have for making cuts in the texts I publish.

But there's something else: my way of finding a word under another word. The word I find is clearer, more precise. I make an incision that liberates what the sentence had buried.

I believe you've come here for my mind as well as my body.

MARIANNE

It's crazy, right? But what do you want me to do, my dear? Throw him out? He's already out. He called this morning.

He leaves messages on the answering machine. No, it's a detox clinic. He's a regular there, it's like he's part of the furniture. Has he stopped drinking? No. I know my Raymond. What? Of course I call him that. I'll say it again: *my* Raymond. Nobody's going to change him. In the future, maybe I'll be . . . yes, that's it, more prudent. But don't talk to me about experience, and don't talk to me about wisdom. I'm broken, Claire. No, I don't want you to come here. Suppose they call you and say you've got a part, what are you going to tell them? "I'm gluing the pieces of my sister back together. She lives with a writer." Part-time writer, full-time boozehound.

Wait, I thought I heard Sarah. No, it wasn't her, it was the neighbors. She's going to come back. She always comes back. What would you want me to tell her? Ten days ago, Raymond cleaned out her bank account, his daughter's bank account. To buy himself some liquor. He cleans out her account and then he says to her, "Where's the respect in this house? Where's your respect for your father?" Three days she's been gone. But she'll come back. "Runaway at fifteen . . ." How does the saying go? "Runaway at fifteen, home to stay at sixteen." Actually, I think I made that up. I invent sentences, they wind up in his short stories. I supply him with dialogue, he breaks a bottle on my head. No, I wasn't flirting. The teachers are . . . affectionate with one another. At our school, in any case. The history professor? That was just to make him jealous. So he'd go into a rage. Oh, that's something I know how to do. Besides, he was drunk. He has a mistress, you know. All . . . all right. Go on if you've got something on the stove. We'll talk later.

*

Hello? Sarah? Who's calling? Who's on the line? You have
to come home now. Come back home. You must come back,
Sarah. Come home.

It's crazy.

DOUGLAS

I need women. Mm-*mm*. Women. I want women. Young,
mature, in the cradle, I don't care. But women.

I never stop telling them that the short story's a feminine
form. She gives you a sidelong glance at the bend of a narrow
lane, and when she disappears you search all over town for
her. Woolf, Mansfield, where *are* those broads?

If I can find ten—ten good stories written by women—
I'll put out my special issue. But I'm never going to find them.
Because I can't put enough money on the table, not all by
myself.

What? Yes, I talked to you about my special issue. Yes I
did, Gerald. I'm calling it *Our Secret Lives*. Or *The Season of
Our Secrets*. No, I'll come up with something better. I'll bring
it out in the fall and blow away the anthologies. They're all
old hat. But the magazine, the magazine will put out its special issue, and that territory will be ours for the next twenty
years. We'll piss on the competition. You and me, Gerald.

You want to know *who* we're going to piss on? I can't
believe it. You don't read the other magazines? Look, I'm

going to beat it across the street. I can cross the street and take an office on the other side. And I can publish novels. I have an offer. Yes, I have an offer. But they don't make my dick hard, Gerald. What makes my dick hard is the magazine. And what I can do with it.

Of course you don't know what I'm talking about, the only reason you come here is to hang paintings. You hang your paintings and I edit the fiction. To each his own. But no, I'm not going across the street. I'm staying here with my rose window.

I'm talking about doubling. About paying twice as much per story as we do now—that way, we attract the best. Yes, it's indispensable. So that they'll accept my cuts. If we double our price, they'll stop flinching. Why do I cut their stories? Why do I rewrite them? Oh, don't talk to me about that . . . Gerald. Don't talk to me about their artistic int . . . their artistic integrity.

I have a magazine to publish. Three short stories per month. Do I have to justify myself? Show my receipts? For God's sake.

I'll give you *one* example. If a short story . . . Gerald. If I buy a story and I'm able to fix it by cutting it a little, or by cutting half of it, well, that's what I do. Here's the thing, though. A great many stories may be excellent except for one problem: a terrible ending. That makes for an awkward situation, because I can't tell the author—I'm simplifying this totally so you'll understand—I can't say, "Your story is good, your ending is bad . . . uh . . . could you rewrite the end?" Because if I say that, every one of them will write another ending even worse than the first, and then I'll be in a real fix, because a relationship, an editorial bond will have been established, and at that stage it would be impolite or incorrect to reject a story they've reworked at my request.

That's why I rewrite them.

Gerald, how do you think I can make them swallow that bitter pill without paying them double?

Yes, I'm a progressive!

I have an ideal in my head. A voice for the magazine. Except I'll never find an author who'll say to me, "Douglas, you're a genius. Rewrite me. You're a god." I'm never going to find that author. But with double the amount of cash on the table, I have a chance to approach my ideal. By constructing it myself.

No, Gerald, it's not a magazine. It's a manifesto. You don't know that because you keep your eyes riveted on those daubs of yours. But if you page through the magazine, you'll yield to the evidence. Those short stories, all together, side by side—that's their voice. Their voice, you understand me?

But it's *my* signature.

RAYMOND

You've reached Marianne and Raymond's house. Please leave a message, we're all ears, and if you're looking for Leo or Sarah, try the soccer field, the video arcade in the middle of town, or even their school. No, on second thought, don't try their school.

"It's me. It's Raymond . . . uh . . . I don't know what to say . . . I'm lost. I'm calling you from a phone booth near the highway. I left the clinic. I took the car, and it broke down.

You know it didn't have a reverse gear anymore, and now the transmission's completely shot. I'm so sorry, Marianne. I don't know who could have done that to you. It was me, of course. I'm stupid. It was me . . . I can see you, you know. I see you on the telephone. Or rather I can imagine you. You're wearing your sister's sweater. Her navy blue sweater. You're holding yourself as straight as the flame of a cigarette lighter. Your hair's hiding your cheekbones. You're rolling a few strands between your fingers. Are you still listening to the same song? I see a glass of something on the coffee table. Magazines all around, a lot of magazines. How can you read that, Marianne? How can you believe in astrology . . . ? And then I see your eyes. Your eyes that catch everything, your wonderful gaze. You're standing at the window, turning the answering machine around, on the lookout for a distant signal. I'd like to be that guy on the horizon signaling to you. Someone you'd be glad to go to. Describe him to me so I can try to be like him. Pick up and describe him to me."

DOUGLAS

What's that? What does that mean, he doesn't want to? Put him on. I'm telling you to put him on. Lorraine . . . Turn the receiver toward him. Ithaca, it's Daddy. Daddy isn't happy. Daddy has to stay at work, he won't be home until late. Mommy's going to have to read you "The Imp of the Perverse." It's going to be Mommy for a change. So you go to bed now, you hear me? Ithaca, stop that shit right now. If you don't go to bed, Daddy's going to come home and cut your balls off. What, Lorraine? I can't? I mustn't? A three-year-old doesn't have balls? My son has . . . Ithaca has . . . oh, all right, you're the boss.

I'll be home by midnight. Midnight or maybe one. I've got three manuscripts to read, I should be there by . . . that's going to depend on . . . on how much cutting I've got to do. No, I have to do it myself. They don't know how. I do it myself. I love you too.

*

If it weren't for Lorraine, I'd forget to go home. I'd spend my life in this office and not even remember that I have a family. Do I have a family? What's it like? Like the magazines lined up on my shelves? Like the stacks of proofs I have to correct? People in my profession take words for flesh. We can hear their hearts beat. We discover a disconcerting kinship with them.

The hour has come. The offices empty out, and I have no more enemies. My rose window switches off. My psoriasis calms down. It's time for my tête-à-tête with the authors.

Outside there's darkness. And a thousand little lights in that darkness, trying to clear a way for themselves. I can't bring them all on board. I'm the Captain of the Storytellers, not the Shipwrecked. You go to sea at your own risk.

However, I'm standing watch. I'm reaching out.

*

I've taken Raymond out of the wastepaper basket. His first sentence has been making me itch since this morning. I don't know why. It didn't have much going for it. Or rather, it had just enough going for it to get stuck in my head.

"Ambulance sirens, that's what I bring home with me from my nights on duty." *Sirens . . . I bring home sirens. From my nights. That's what I br . . . I bring home sirens from my nights.* Why use more words? Raymond brings home sirens from his nights. That's all. The reader understands.

"From midnight to eight in the morning, the sirens follow one another, or sometimes blend together, on the two-lane road that circles . . ." Uh-oh. *They blend around the hospital,* period. "I can hear them from my night-watchman's box, first far, then close, and finally not at all, when . . ." More itching. Pruritus. Pruritus between two commas. ". . . when the lights are still on but the sound is off and the ambulances park in the back, unburdened of an injured person or a corpse." Don't you see that "the back" equals "exile" equals "death"? Either you choose the back or you choose death. You have too much heart, Raymond. *When they park in the back, I can hear them from my night-watchman's box.* "At the moment, my thoughts go no farther than that." Why "at the moment"? You're already there, in the moment. "To me, emergencies are distant sounds . . ."—argh, *distant,* an adjective, a scale—"I hear from inside a glass cage." That has to go, zip, all of it.

So what are we left with?

I bring home sirens from my nights. Paragraph. *They blend around the hospital. When they park in the back, I can hear them from my night-watchman's box. My thoughts go no farther than that. Emergencies are sounds I hear from inside a glass cage.* Paragraph.

Not one word too many. A single comma, after the parking lot in the back, which is death.

Raymond, I'm starting to like you.

*

Hello, Lorraine? It's me. Don't wait up.

RAYMOND |

I can't hear you. I can't hear you very well. I'm . . . The telephone's right next to the coffeemaker. No, a diner on the highway.

Raymond, yes. Paula gave . . . A friend gave me your message. I just got it.

We've met, you know. We used to work for the same editor. School textbooks, right. I compiled excerpts from short stories. But the company did some reshuffling and I got laid off. It's me, Raymond. May I call you Douglas?

Right, I've sent you some . . . I've sent you a bunch of stories. Ten at least, maybe twenty. Yes, I should have mentioned it. I didn't think you . . . I didn't think you'd remember who I was.

You read one? Which? "Who Needs Air?" Mm-hmm. Ah. But you're calling it what? "Compartment." Sure, why not? "The Compartment," then. Oh, I see. A single word. "Compartment."

So you're accepting it? I can't hear you. I'm sorry, it's the coffee ma—

What do you mean, "No"?

Why are you cutting it if you're not going to accept it?

Well, what are you taking out, exactly? Then . . . then what are you *keeping*? The argument. Nothing but the argument? You reduced the first three pages to a paragraph? And that doesn't work. Mm-hmm.

But then don't take it, I don't give a shit. How much? You're paying twice as much as . . . ? I see. Yeah.

So you would cut the end. You'd cut the beginning and the end. Yes, it would be shorter like that. How far in? But that's the middle! That's right in the middle of the argument! "Always cut off arguments in the middle." No, I've never heard that. And your students listen to you? Well yes, of course, that means there's less to write. If they all stop in the middle . . .

Hello? Mr. Douglas?

God damn it.

*

Hello, it's me, it's Raymond. We were cut off. You hung up? You were finished. That was all you wanted to tell me? No, I'm going to sell it somewhere else. All right, I'll think about it. Yes, I'll send you others. I've got a whole raft of arguments. They're my specialty. And thanks!

Asshole.

RAYMOND |

There aren't any blinds on the windows in this motel. I lie unmoving, with my eyes wide open. The neon sign projects a turquoise-blue light onto the ceiling. Unless it's the reflection of the swimming pool.

I call up Marianne every hour. I leave a message and wait for her to pick up. When she does, even if she doesn't say anything, even if she just breathes into the phone, I'll know I can go back home.

I can't sleep. I turn on the TV. A film about a blind skater, a young girl. The story's easy to follow, with or without the sound. But my thoughts are elsewhere. I'm thinking about "Compartment." I don't call it "Who Needs Air?" anymore. I imagine my story in Douglas's version.

The one that stops in the middle.

"Close the window, Robin."

"It's stifling in here."

"Close the window, the kids are going to catch colds."

She stubs out her cigarette. While she's lighting up another one—the ashtray is overflowing, how can she have any left?—I pivot and lift the window higher.

"I'm stifling, me!"

When I turn around, there's no anger on her face. She comes close to me. Cigarette in hand, she puts her arms around me and lays her forehead against my chest.

I hear the TV, the muffled voices, and a crying child.

"Theo," I murmur.

She raises her head. We freeze and listen.

Marion leaves the kitchen.

I should follow her, but I can't move. I think about the secret compartment in the fridge. About all the compartments in all the fridges in the neighborhood. Everybody should have one, I say to myself. A secret place, there or somewhere else.

I say that to myself, and I start shaking.

End of the story. Three cuts with the scissors, a few sentences moved around. And Marianne and I are a little more separated, a little more cut off from each other.

Is that the way you see us, Douglas? You're mistaken. Some hope has to remain, some source of light. Even if it's only a neon sign on the side of the highway.

It's a good thing he didn't want my story.

Even though I could've used the money . . . I could have . . . I could . . . He edits the most widely read magazine in the country.

I can send him other stories. What have I got to lose?

MARIANNE

Why did I pick up? Why did I pick up that telephone?

I'm not sure they pulled all the bottle fragments out of my head. A shard must have remained under my skin. And now it's circulating through my veins, poisoning me in small doses. I'll spit it out one day. I'll spit out the debris of our love.

But I'm not ready. The proof is what I thought when I heard him: *How's he going to tell the bottle story? What will he weave around it? What name will he give me? Emma, I'd like to be called Emma. Or Rita, why not? The story he tells had better be successful. In case it's our last.*

That's what I thought, and then I picked up the phone.

RAYMOND

A stranger in my house, that's what I am.

I've been sleeping in the living room ever since I came back home. Marianne has quarantined me. Sarah's back home too. Until the next time she runs away. Meanwhile she leaves early in the morning for the drugstore, where she works as a cashier. She tells us her classes begin at noon. We know it's not true, but we don't say anything. It's still early when Marianne starts moving around the kitchen and wakes me up. Sleeping on the sofa hurts my back, but I don't complain. A man must earn his place in the marital bed.

Leo's a tranquil teenager. He doesn't smoke, doesn't drink, doesn't run away. The complete opposite of his sister. Maybe at twenty he'll become a psychopath. "You should have more fun," I tell him. "Enjoy life." His reply: "Don't have time for that. I'm in too much of a hurry to get the hell out of here." That kid's got ambition. He takes after his parents.

Marianne and I haven't shelved our hopes. I've done some arithmetic: For eleven years we've been going from one little job to another, from town to campus, from training courses to night school. By this time, I could have a medical degree. I could be—who knows?—a cardiologist. Except that I've never examined any heart but my own, and I give no prescriptions. My sole recommendation: "Keep the faith, and a bottle within reach."

I go out into the yard. I run my eyes over the house, peering through the sliding glass doors. People are moving about from one room to another. They speak to one another and occasionally address me. They move their lips as though warning me of some danger.

I've come back but I don't feel at home.

*

I had another call from Douglas. He's clamoring for more short stories. He thinks I'm talented, he thinks I've got something in my belly, but he can't say what. "Guts?" I said jokingly. There was a silence, and then he tossed out, "If you've got some guts, send 'em to me."

I looked over my stories again. Some are more than ten years old. I'm capable of lugging a short story around for years and years. I correct it, I grow older with it, and most of the time, it improves. My life remains the same or goes into a little more of a spin, but my stories improve.

Perfection in what I write; chaos in all the rest.

I sent Douglas the lot. Even if he takes only one, I'll be happy. Let him put just one of my stories in his magazine and pay me for my efforts. Let me finally be paid for something I've written.

That's all I hope for. The guy isn't God. Just an editor.

Someone who has a vital need to hear good stories. He'll go looking for them all the way to the end of the night.

I looked outside. All the lights were off. I imagined a map showing our house, our yard, a wilderness, and then the city—the metropolis, streaked by the moving headlights of its traffic. High up, one window, one single window, shines in the darkness. It's Douglas, reading my stories.

That window hasn't left my mind since.

I put my typewriter on the kitchen table and started typing.

The refrigerator was vibrating so hard it seemed it would die. I got up and struck it a heavy blow. It went back to its ordinary hum.

In all likelihood, it's not long for this world.

MARIANNE |

Raymond? An envelope came for you. It filled the whole mailbox and all my mail wound up on the ground. Mom's letter was lying in a puddle. What's in this envelope? Did you order some magazines? The sender is . . . "Douglas." Douglas something. Who's he?

Raymond, will you please stop typing for five minutes? Click clack click clack! I'm going nuts from so much clicking and clacking.

Open it, my hands are wet.

Well?

You're about to burn yourself with your cigarette.

RAYMOND AND MARIANNE

Marianne and I are in the kitchen. She's holding my stories in her hand. My stories, revised and corrected by Douglas.

"So what do you think?" I ask her.

"He did more than just cut. I read the first two and skimmed the others."

"Well, you know them."

"As if I'd written them. Do they all do this?"

"Who?"

"Magazine types. Book editors don't take so many liberties, do they?"

"A magazine has more constraints."

"What constraints?"

"Advertising. They need space for the ads."

"You mean to say this guy cuts down your stories to make room for ads?"

"He didn't cut all of them. Look at 'Why Are You Crying?' It's intact."

"Except that now it's called 'Biscuits.'"

"He loves one-word titles."

"And 'Excuse Me' has become 'Collision.'"

"One or the other, he said. I can keep it 'Excuse Me' if I want."

"Are you going to keep it?"

"Marianne, he knows his job."

"You told me they call him 'Scissors.'"

"It's a compliment. It means he has a good eye."

"Do *you* think he does?"

"Nothing's definite. He's proposing some cuts. I can do what I want about them."

"That's my question. What are you going to do about these proposed cuts?"

"Marianne, I don't believe you realize what's going on. Getting published in that magazine—I know some people who would crawl on the earth for that."

"But not you. Right?"

"He knows his job."

"'Biscuits' . . . 'Collision' . . . 'Scissors.'"

She kept on muttering. I got up and opened the fridge. I took a beer, the only one left.

Her voice suddenly got louder: "Did he really say you have too much heart?"

DOUGLAS

The throes of departure. I'm accustomed to them. All writers know the feeling. At the moment when they're about to jump on board, they imagine the worst. As if I was going to shipwreck their stories.

Raymond got worried. The cuts frightened him. He thinks his short stories are going to turn into . . . very thinly sliced Raymond.

That's not what my scissors do. The writers I bring on board know it. They know it, and they thank me.

Take Raymond, since we're talking about him. Take his story about a woman who feels repulsion for her husband. She's lying down in her bedroom. When her husband climbs into bed and scoots close to put his arms around her, Raymond writes that she "moves" her legs. Too predictable, much too timorous. I strike "moves" and put "spreads." *She spreads her legs.*

Sometimes Raymond's as modest as a silly young girl.

MARIANNE AND RAYMOND

"Is that what you meant to say, Raymond? You meant to say 'spreads'?"

"I don't know what I meant to say."

"Then how can he? How can Douglas know that for you?"

"Maybe I thought 'spreads' and then wrote 'moves.' It's true that I have a tendency not to say things."

"That's a virtue, right? Chekhov, Salinger—you always say their force comes from not saying things."

"In *their* work. In their work, it's a force."

"And in yours?"

"It might be a weakness."

DOUGLAS

Raymond has a strange way of ending his stories. It's like when another driver stalls out in front of you at a green light. You don't wait for him to restart his engine. You steer around him and pass him by. That was my first reaction to Raymond's work.

The second, no, the third time I read through it, I understood. I no longer saw any clumsiness in the way he stalled. I perceived that the fulfillment of his short stories was in that very stalling.

Yes, Raymond's art lies in stalling in front of your eyes when you least expect it.

I get out of my car and walk over to his old jalopy. I open the passenger door and get in. Raymond's eyes are blurry with alcohol. I grab the steering wheel with my left hand and say, "Onward."

Have confidence, Raymond. Onward.

We're going to travel down a stretch of road together.

And we'll both stall when we feel like it.

I look in the rearview mirror and see my car with nobody at the wheel. I have no regrets. The gas tank was practically empty.

MARIANNE

Go. He's paying for your ticket, you may as well go. But don't drink in front of him, okay? And tell him you want to keep "Excuse Me" as the title for your story. If that's what you want. I don't even know anymore.

Of course I'm happy, of course I'm excited.

But don't discuss our debts, all right? Be sure you don't say a word about our money problems.

DOUGLAS

Lately I've had my doubts. First of all, there's Lorraine, talking to me about divorce. I take her at her word and call up the best lawyer in town. I didn't expect to find she'd hired him two days previously.

And then there's Nicole, that whore. I discover the best female short-story writer of her generation, and what does she do? She signs an exclusive contract with the outfit across the street to publish her novels. I say to her, "Nicole, your name is Ingratitude." She replies, "No, it's Nicole." Novelists are too prosaic.

I wished her good luck, but because of her departure, I hit an air pocket. My scissors were snipping at the void. Then Raymond came. With his fondness for whiskey. In his case, alcohol and writing make a compatible couple. Until alcohol prevails. Then he loses all restraint. He says too much when he ought to say less. He sounds like someone who wants to be forgiven. But nobody forgives too many words.

When I'm editing Raymond, a strange phenomenon occurs: I see Douglas through him. *All his secrets are mine.* When I edit Raymond, I have no more doubt.

He was supposed to have arrived in town by now. He was supposed to be in this office.

Hello, Sibyll? Why isn't he here yet?

46

MARIANNE

My head's spinning. The colors in the bar I work in clash so hard it hurts. Every day I go from the school where I'm a student teacher to the bar where I'm a waitress. This morning I handed out plastic letters to the kids. Then I waited patiently until they managed to spell "CONSEQUENCE." While waiting, I considered the best way of illustrating that word. "As a *consequence* of my marriage to an alcoholic writer, I have two totally unrelated jobs and a feeling of vertigo when I go from one to the other." I didn't tell them that—I would have been fired on the spot—but the sentence has stuck in my head and leads to other sentences. "For the moment, everything that Raymond writes remains of no *consequence*; he might as well copy out a mail order catalogue. But maybe his meeting with this editor, this high mucky-muck, will have some *consequences*, who knows?" I'm still not finished with that word when I find myself pouring hot coffee and trying hard not to splash the red, yellow, and fuchsia leatherette wall seats. "As a *consequence* of his misdeeds, the interior decorator should be hanged." A greasy smell permeates the fibers of my apron, the straps of my top, the locks of my hair. I feel like slapping that customer down there with his elbows on the bar—I can't stand the way he lets his coffee get cold and looks as though his house has just been seized—but I've got to watch the little old freezer repairman, whose eyes aren't anywhere near focused. Look at him, a miracle, he manages to hold on to the stool. I don't want to have to lift him out of the beer puddles on the floor again today. I replace the coffeepot and switch on the percolator. Nobody complains about the noise—everybody's as numb as I am. Only three hours to go.

I notice a couple I didn't see come in. Two young people sitting in a booth and facing each other. They look as though they just had a fight. They're like Ray and me right before we got married, when I was several weeks pregnant. The girl's a bit plump, the way I was at sixteen. She's sitting back with her arms folded. Looking at her, you'd say she feels she's being accused.

I see their lips moving, and I have the impression I'm listening to us.

"You want them both. Why compare them, why put them in competition with each other?"

"Marianne—"

"You can want to write and you can want our baby."

"But I couldn't choose. I'd be forced to—"

"Not forced, no. You wouldn't have to force yourself."

"If I was obliged to choose between my family and my writing, I believe I'd choose—"

"You can have both."

"I'd choose writing."

I look at the girl. Her face is set. She's very close to standing up, walking through the bar, and going out. Why shouldn't she have a choice? Why not her too? Holding back tears, she looks over at the door.

Then she turns to the boy. "I can make it work. You'll see. Everything will go so well you won't have to choose."

She falls silent. She's just sealed her fate. Let no one say this fate was reserved for her at her birth, that it's the *conse-*

quence of her sex and her upbringing. Let no one say that. It's the consequence of nothing but her love.

In that case, why do the blinds on the front window make her think of prison bars?

The boy leans over and kisses her.

"I love you so much, Marianne. You'll never know how much I love you."

I choose that moment to approach their booth, coffeepot in hand.

"All right, you two, what's your pleasure?"

RAYMOND AND DOUGLAS

"You visit them?"

"Of course."

"But not when they're so far away? Not as far as where I live?"

"Sometimes even farther."

"Really?"

"If it's necessary. Only if it's necessary."

"When is it necessary?"

"When I want to prevent them from going over to the competition. How do you think a person becomes one of the three editors that count in this town?"

"I had no idea."

"You're not going to eat your sushi?"

"I don't know if sushi's my thing."

"I'll eat it for you. Have you brought the manuscript?"

"The one you mailed me?"

49

"We're going to keep it the way it is now, all right?"

"Well . . . I mean . . . I discussed it with Marianne."

"Marianne?"

"She's my wife."

"I didn't know you were married."

"I married Marianne when she was sixteen."

"I got married three times in sixteen years. You don't want your beer?"

"You can have it."

"My divorce comes through next week."

"Marianne finds the cuts—"

"Lorraine thinks I spend too much time at my office."

"She finds the cuts, the cuts in my short stories—"

"Raymond. Let me stop you right away. Writers' wives are their worst enemy."

"They are?"

"Especially when they're dead."

"Why?"

"Because they get it into their heads that they must protect their husband's work."

"And they do it wrong?"

"It's a profession. Just like widowhood's a profession. But it's not the same profession."

"Being a widow's a profession?"

"Being a writer's widow is. A writer's widow is a full-time manager of her late husband's posterity. It turns into an obsession. Such women lose all judgment and make some . . . disastrous decisions. What does Marianne know about editing short stories?"

"Oh, uh, she's a schoolteacher."

"..."

"And also a waitress, to pay the rent. Supplemental income."

"What does she know about editing?"

"We've talked about my stories together."

"They're extraordinary, those stories of yours!"

"Thanks."

"The only one I left out is 'Why Are You Crying?' I didn't have time to look at it closely."

"But you changed the title."

"I have to read it again."

"I hope you like it."

"Not to worry, not to worry. Let's go back to—"

"Your cuts."

"We don't know each other very well. Our paths crossed a long time ago, and we've just gotten back into contact."

"Lucky for me."

"And we haven't done anything yet, the two of us. We haven't yet accomplished anything."

"Still, you're one of the three editors—"

"Every time I publish a story, I put my reputation on the line."

"Really?"

"If only writers . . . if they would only see things my way, there wouldn't be all this waste."

"Waste?"

"These obese books, this useless fat. You know what they call me? 'The Captain of—'"

"'Scissors,' they call you. Is that a compliment?"

"No. It's resentment. It's misplaced pride."

"Ah."

"The author's worst enemy."

"Along with his widow."

"Along with his wife, Raymond. His wife who interferes in the editing process. What do you think of these stories?"

"Which ones?"

"These here."

"The short version."

"Don't say 'version.' Don't say 'short.' Take them as they are."

"They're not how they were. They're—"

"Another beer, Miss Lovely!"

"I was going to say 'drained of sap.'"

"You were going to say it. You said it."

"Marianne thinks so too."

"I'd like to know her. I'd like to meet her. You all could come to dinner with Lorraine and . . . no, wait, I'm getting divorced next week."

"Marianne thinks about it the way I do. She'd tell you the same thing."

"I have a different idea of sap, Raymond. Different from yours and Marianne's."

"We could make a compromise."

"Of course, because I'm very fond of these stories."

"We could come to an understanding about the cuts."

"After all, you want to be published . . . no need to say anything, of course you do. Who doesn't dream of being published? Who? Tell me who."

"Nobody I know."

"And when you're not writing and not drinking, you go trout fishing, you said? The countryside, what a blessing."

MARIANNE

I should have kept my mouth shut. Now he feels trapped. I used to think . . . I thought he wanted my opinion. He always asks me for it. I've often thought that if he ever reached anything like the beginning of a success, I'd be there to encourage him. Just as I was there to support him when nothing was working. So what do I tell him when I see those cuts? I say, "You're going to stand up for yourself, aren't you? You're not going to give in?" As if he was getting ready to betray me. I wanted to defend his writing. I've been defending his writing for ten years, for ten years I've been supporting him . . . There were so many words crossed out. Not just words, not just sentences, but whole pages. As if Raymond's short stories were made up of a few words and many long silences. But his stories, they're him. They're him spilling out. Who does this Douglas think he is? He says—he dared to say, "You have too much heart, Raymond." As if he was going to have to relieve him of some of it.

Nobody wants his stories, so he feels trapped. If he refuses to accept the cuts, he loses a chance of being published. And we lose the money. But if he gives in, he's going to feel like a coward.

In the past, there was Raymond, me, and between us,

Raymond's writing. Now there's someone else. Douglas and his magazine. Is there any room left for me?

Is that what I've become, one person too many?

RAYMOND |

Suppose he's right? Suppose he sees something I can't see? Because there's too much of me in there, too much of my life in every one of my stories. Douglas sees a writer in me. He doesn't talk to me like he's talking to a drunk. But in Marianne's eyes, there's nothing I can do, I see myself as a drunkard, I see myself as a nasty guy. A bastard whose stories make him better.

Another Scotch, please!

Being far from Marianne doesn't agree with me. This town doesn't agree with me, either. Everybody here looks as though they're right.

As soon as someone starts talking around here, I get the impression it's to lay the blame on me.

THE UNKNOWN WOMAN AND RAYMOND |

"Why come into a bar if you want to be alone?"

"I beg your pardon?"

"I've been watching you for the past few minutes. You talked to yourself the whole time. What's your name?"

"Raymond."

"What do you do for a living? You sell cars?"

"More like spare parts."

"You see? I've got a sixth sense. I knew you were going to sell me something."

"I didn't say I had anything to—"

"My car broke down outside. You could start it."

". . ."

"No?"

"I can always try."

MARIANNE

Hello? Hello, I . . . I called an hour ago. Room number six. He's still not there? And he didn't leave his key at the desk? All right.

I have to tell you . . . I was very moved when I heard your voice. I haven't stopped thinking about it. You have my mother's voice, if she were black. She's sick at the moment. Of course, you're right, I hear her voice everywhere. But yours is special. No, don't say that, you're not just anybody. You're special. You have understanding.

It's one o'clock in the morning and he's still not back. He hasn't returned to his room. Should I call the police? No, of course not. They'd laugh in my face. Sometimes Raymond, I mean my husband, doesn't come home at night. That's no reason to call the police. Especially as he may well be in a cell, sleeping off his liquor. But that's here. In a big city, it's another story. Every hour he's gone . . . well, you understand me. I appreciate your voice and the fact that you haven't hung up on me. I appreciate it more than you think.

Right, that's what I have to tell myself. He's with a man, the editor he went to see. If he's not with him, he must be in a bar, and what can happen to him in a bar? Doesn't a man alone in a big city have a right to the comfort of bars?

But truly, if my mother were black, she'd have your voice.

RAYMOND

Her name's Jeanine. I wasn't able to start her car. Now she's calling me "Smooth Talker." She invited me to spend the night with her. To seek her forgiveness, she said. I could tell by her tense face that it would be best for me to accept. I didn't have enough money left for cab fare anyway.

She lives in the suburbs. A gabled house with tall guillotine windows.

"Have a seat, Smooth Talker."

She served me one beer and then another. A little later, I found myself in her bed. The bedroom was upstairs. The wallpaper looked about a hundred years old. In front of the bed was a chest of drawers with a three-paneled mirror on top. My toes were reflected in the central panel.

Jeanine stayed in the bathroom a long time. I heard her cursing the pipes. I said, "Plumbing problems?"

I saw my toes moving in the mirror.

"Goddamned pipes!"

I sat up straight. She came out of the bathroom. A strange

smell accompanied her. A scent of dried flowers, Jeanine's smell.

Some branches projected their shadows onto the curtain. There must have been a big garden outside. She came close to me. She put her hand on my penis and I thought, *Petunias*. A story came together in my head.

I don't know how long I slept. When I opened my eyes, she was lying on the edge of the bed with her back turned to me. I ran my eyes up the length of her spinal column. It was like a delicate mechanism nestled under the surface of her skin.

She heard my breathing.

"What do you know how to do, Smooth Talker?"

I searched for a reply.

"What can you do with your hands?"

"Oh, a lot of things."

"For example?"

"Pick a trade, any trade. You'll see—I've done every sort of work."

"Except for auto mechanic."

"Except for that, I admit."

It seemed to me that she was smiling. I encouraged her: "Well? Pick one."

"Basketball player."

"Good guess!"

"Professional?"

"Semiprofessional."

That wasn't entirely false. At the university, I replaced a player on the school team. I rode the bench the whole time, but I was a substitute all the same.

"Cardiologist?"

"No. But night watchman in a hospital."

She looked interested.

"It had a cardiology department . . . People of any age can have a fragile heart. That's one of the things I learned in that hospital."

She was smoking a cigarette, and she held it out to me.

I kept on trotting out my employment history. When I revealed that I'd been a plumber, she sat up straight and said, "I need a plumber!"

She grabbed my wrist and pulled me into the bathroom. A monkey wrench and some bolts were lying on the shower mat.

I spent the rest of the night clearing the bathroom pipes of the clumps of earth that were blocking them. She had no idea how clumps of earth had gotten in there.

I learned later that Jeanine was a flight attendant. A flight attendant who lived alone in a gabled house with a garden around it. The garden threatened to invade the house.

I told myself I'd put that in "Petunias."

MARIANNE |

I thought I didn't give a damn about that. I thought it wasn't important. "He can sleep with whomever he wants," I said. "I don't care. All I have to do is sleep with someone else myself."

I slept with the history teacher. It did me no good. I could sleep with the principal and his assistant. By way of climbing up the social ladder.

"There are twenty ways of climbing up the social ladder." That's what you told me when you refused to let me complete my education.

The education I didn't complete because you were getting yours.

The education I stopped because you wanted to write.

The education I interrupted when Leo got sick.

The education I couldn't finish because you were too fidgety to stay in one place.

The education I suspended when they fired you from the warehouse.

The education I abandoned because you were drinking.

The education I envied you for getting.

The education I would have been better at getting than you.

My education.

It took me eleven years to obtain my certificate. "Become a teacher and we'll go from campus to campus," you said. You were thinking only about yourself, about the writing workshops you wanted to be in. Now you're a better, a much better writer. And me, I'm a teacher during the day and a waitress at night. For tips that don't pay one percent of the mortgage on this house.

How we used to love each other, though. Madly, like the couple in the film we watched yesterday. A girl and a boy meet during a traveling carnival. They get married, live it up for a while, and run through all their money. Their only remaining choice is to hold up banks. It reminded me of us. Except we're not gangsters. And I can't see you holding up anything, except maybe a liquor store.

Almost five o'clock. I can't sleep. I polished the furniture—
rubbed it so hard it's shining like the surface of a pond. I'd
like to slip into that pond and go under. When you're floating
on your back and the water's lapping at your ears, you can
sense the slightest quivering.

Everything that's in you.

The sound of jet engines. An airplane taking off. It's as if
there's no more distance between us. And I take off too.

Petunias

When Robert returned home from his third consecutive day in town, he found his wife lying on the wall-to-wall carpet. Her legs were rigid, her arms outspread. She was staring at the ceiling.

"Darling, did you fall down?"

No reply. He noticed that his wife's cheeks were sunken, as though sucked from inside.

He reached for the telephone on the coffee table in the living room. "Do you . . . do you want me to call someone?"

A doctor, a neighbor lady, or as a last resort his mother-in-law.

"Put that receiver down, you son of a bitch!"

The words came out as though a ventriloquist, or the devil in person, had taken possession of his wife.

"Ah, you're breathing," he said with relief.

He hung up the receiver.

Emma got up and went into the kitchen, which was separated from the living room by a yellow ceramic bar. A long time ago, working together, the two of them had glued on the little mosaic tiles. Robert had wanted to figure a white swan on the front of the bar. Emma had thought it would be a big deal just to get all the tiles glued in place. In the end she'd finished the job herself, without depicting any swan.

She busied herself at the kitchen sink. When she looked over at Robert, her eyes were furious. He thought it was because he'd come home so late.

"I'm sorry."

He was the first to recognize his errors—a trait that exasperated his wife. She would have preferred a husband who was arrogant and obstinate like all other husbands but who would have had the nerve to look her in the face.

She muttered through clenched teeth, "If you think I'm just going to let this pass . . ."

She was peeling some potatoes. Considering the state she was in, Robert was afraid her fingers would slip and she'd cut herself. He dismissed his mental image of the peeler slicing his wife's wrists to shreds.

For some time now, Emma had been on edge. Especially since Robert, an unpublished author, had started commuting to the city more and more often under the pretext that he needed the urban atmosphere in order to write.

They lived near a highway access road in what looked like a village. Small farms alternated with moderately priced rental houses, each with its own yard. The place gave the impression of being far from everything. Robert would jump on the morning express and return in the evening on the 5:48 (except for this time, when he'd taken the next train).

Upon his return, when Emma would question him, he wouldn't talk about his book. He seemed to have nothing to say about the city. Vexed by his silence, she'd ask him, "But at least you liked it, right?"

He'd make a face before eventually saying, "I wonder if I'm not a country writer." The situation had been going on for five months.

She flung a utensil into the sink and began kneading her hair with her wet hands. "It's the last straw, Robert!" she said, yelling the words. "The last straw!"

She left the bar and went back to the living room, where she lay down again, weeping and pounding the carpet with her fists.

Robert understood that the last straw wasn't the fact that he'd come home sixty minutes later than usual but the mistress he'd been seeing in the city for the last five months.

While Emma remained stretched out on the living-room floor, he opened the sideboard cabinet and poured himself a glass of whiskey.

Had Emma been having him tailed? Followed to Jeannette's place? Jeannette was the flight attendant he'd met in a bar. He could see her house, with its gables, its second-story window, and the warm light that shined, behind the curtain, on their frolics. The memory made him feel ashamed.

He sipped his drink for a while and then said, "Are you trying to tell me something?" He was standing on the living-room threshold with his whiskey glass in his hand. He didn't go any farther into the room for fear of tripping over his wife. "Say something, for God's sake! Let's settle this once and for all!"

She'd covered her eyes with a mask, one of those sleep masks airlines hand out to passengers on long-haul flights. Robert thought Emma was making a veiled allusion to the flight attendant. Emma lifted the mask, stared at him, contorted her mouth, and put the mask back in place. Then she said, "I don't want to settle anything. I just want revenge, you bastard."

"Why do you have that mask on?"

"So I won't have to see your ugly mug."

He turned on his heels and went up the stairs.

He was on the last step when he heard Emma say, "My own Robert . . ." This was followed by a snigger, and then by sobbing.

He heaved a sigh. In the love notes she scribbled on the backs of oblong postcards—watercolors of airport terminals—Jeannette addressed him as "My own Robert." Why had he brought home one of those cards? Whenever the living room started running short of ashtrays and glasses, Emma would go into his study to retrieve the ones he'd left there. While gathering them up, she'd cast rapid glances at the page in his typewriter and the papers lying around.

Robert knew how to recognize a subconsciously deliberate mistake. Leaving that postcard by his typewriter was the same as asking to be discovered; he'd *wanted* to introduce chaos into his household.

He thought back to their wedding day. To avoid expense, they'd been married in a public park. Emma and Robert were broke, but they had all kinds of ambitions. Ambitions that had never flourished. Two children born too soon and a grueling series of menial jobs, not to mention his chronic alcoholism—all that had darkened their horizon and invaded their home like weeds.

Robert loved watching his children grow up. Cathy looked like her father, and Victor had his mother's features. Robert found this gender inversion charming, like a stylistic device. But beneath his pride in being a dad, anxiety was bubbling. The incessant attention the children required— Emma could take care of them only in the evening, after she came home from work—hadn't that constricted his talent?

One night, after he'd finished knocking back a bottle of
gin, Robert thought he heard strange sounds coming from
Cathy and Victor's room. The sole illumination in the hall
was a night-light. The red halo it cast on the floor glowed
like a burning ember. He groped his way down the hall.
The children's names, scrawled in chalk, danced on a little
blackboard hung on their door. He went in.

After his eyes adjusted to the darkness, he still couldn't
make out the bodies under the covers, but he noticed the
slow movements of creepers and branches. They made
sucking noises as they expanded, meandered, coiled around
the curtain rods. His children had changed shapes. They'd
become those knotty branches, powerful, loaded with sap,
growing from second to second in a greenhouse room too
cramped to contain them.

Robert's heart started pounding in his chest. He heard
the snap of the wall switch, and the room was flooded
with light. Cathy and Victor were sound asleep. There was
nothing unusual in the room. He turned around and saw his
wife, who was sternly looking him up and down.

"Never come in here when you've been drinking, you
hear me?"

She pushed him out into the hall and closed the door in
his face, remaining alone with the children in their room, in
the greenhouse where they were mysteriously growing.

Years had passed, Cathy and Victor were in their early
teens, and measles and chicken pox had given way to other
worries: Cathy would stay out all night without permission,
and Victor never went out at all.

As for Robert, his penchant for drink remained

undiminished, and he was away from home more and more frequently. The flight attendant was only the most recent of his infidelities.

Now that he'd approached the point of no return, he was obliged to "choose between the city and the country," as Emma put it. He decided to suspend work on his novel.

With spring in the air, he would turn to gardening.

He verified the state of his continually overdrawn account, withdrew a little money, and bought himself a pair of rubber boots. Blue denim overalls completed his outfit. There was a shed in the back of the yard, and he remembered seeing some gardening tools on the workbench in there. He took stock of them.

The state the tools were in, their age and wear, revealed that the yard had a history. The rake looked like a museum piece. The hoe could fall apart on him at any moment. Robert set about learning how to handle those blunt, rough instruments.

Previously he'd looked upon his yard as a piece of waste ground. He'd go back there to smoke, keeping his eyes on the sky so he wouldn't have to see the brush at his feet. It had grown anarchically in recent months. Robert wrote in his journal that he detected *enmity* in the yard—the italics, which he had a tendency to overuse in his short stories, were justified in this case by the way the weeds advanced, proliferated, encroached upon the family home.

He tackled the most urgent task first: weeding the flower beds. The hoe didn't fall apart on him. There was a lot of rain in early April that year. Rain, Robert discovered, made uprooting things easier, but he didn't find that method fast enough. He sought out information about weed killers and saw that one was praised above all others. He bought a supply of it.

There was a hydrangea growing in the back of the yard. The plant dated from the period when Emma had yielded to a transient gardening impulse. Robert noticed that the hydrangea was being smothered by brambles. The ease with which he removed them, thus giving the flower its first taste of freedom, surprised him. A man who refused to make cuts in his writing, a man prepared to keep weak sentences despite the detriment they did to the whole, was discovering the nonnegotiable laws of nature. Either you eradicated the weeds, or the flower died altogether.

Robert realized that gardening could make him a better writer. But he wasn't writing anymore. He spent his days in the yard.

At dinner, while Emma was serving Cathy and Victor portions of steak, Robert was neither melancholy nor sullen. He felt a need to communicate his intuitions. Presuming that his son and daughter were old enough to be interested in all things, he expounded his idea to them: "A weed is a plant that's not in its proper place. It would be proper in a meadow, but it's improper in a garden. You have to have the courage to pull it up. By the roots. A yard, and especially a garden, must not be abandoned to nature. If you let it go, it will soon be nothing but brush land."

Cathy and Victor counted the minutes until they'd be allowed to leave the dinner table. Emma didn't say a word. But when her husband picked up his fork, she exclaimed, "Robert, your hands are all muddy!"

The teens burst out laughing. Robert had to go and wash his hands, as if he'd regressed to the time of his childhood.

He next devoted himself to composting. There were two kinds of compost; the kind you buy in stores and nurseries, and the kind you made yourself. This discovery delighted Robert. Cut brush, peelings, tea leaves, coffee grounds—they all mingled together behind the toolshed, decomposed into humus, and were returned to the earth. Less waste, less stuff inexorably headed for the dump.

The more he planted and spaded and planted again, the more stones rose up from the depths of the soil.

One evening, over dessert, he declared, "The movement of things in general is from the earth to the sky."

Victor stood up and said, "Math homework."

Emma went to the window to have a cigarette. She stared into space, exhaling puffs of smoke. Robert tried to catch his wife's eye but couldn't.

Ever since he'd thrown himself heart and soul into gardening, his family had looked at him as though he were some sort of strange animal. How could he make them understand that the only goal of all that activity was to bring him closer to them?

For some time, Emma had been coming home later and later. At first Robert hadn't paid much attention. But one evening when his wife returned flushed and slightly disheveled, he remembered her words: *I don't want to settle anything. I just want revenge, you bastard.*

It was after midnight. Emma was asleep upstairs. As for Robert, he couldn't sleep. He was in the yard, pacing back and forth and considering the hypothesis of his wife's lover.

In the darkness, he smelled more than saw the flowers that embellished the lawn. Very early in the spring, he'd seized the opportunity to plant petunias, but he was surprised they'd bloomed so soon. From where he stood, he could inhale their faint but pervasive fragrance.

An idea came to him. Tomorrow, as early as possible, he'd get his wife involved in the renewal of their garden. They'd plant things together on their scant acre of land and recycle their missteps, their remorse—all the compost accumulated between them.

"Darling, does our garden have any importance for you?"

Emma put down her still-steaming cup. "But yes . . . it always has."

"Has it?"

"When we moved here, we promised we'd replant the garden together."

Emma lowered her eyes. Those days were long gone.

"I'm sorry," Robert said.

Emma looked at him as though she thought he was going to tell her about another flight attendant.

"I've taken the garden too much to heart, I haven't left you any room. I'd like—"

"I'm going to be late."

She stopped short. Robert had taken her hand. He ran his

thumb over her fingers as though brushing petals. He said, "I'd like you to help me replant the garden."

Emma gently withdrew her hand. She nodded to him, swallowed a last mouthful, and left.

A few seconds later, he heard the car start. He felt serene, well on the way to saving his marriage.

He walked out to the garden. "Those petunias are a mistake," he thought, inhaling their fragrance.

A few days later, a Sunday, the yard was drenched in sunlight, and Emma and Victor were stirring the compost. A sudden interest in gardening had seized the teenager. Intent on removing the ivy from a low wall, Robert listened with one ear to the exchange between his wife and son.

"You have to turn over the compost so the grass won't stagnate," she said. "Here, turn it over with this spade."

"Like that?"

"Dig deeper. Really hump it!"

Victor started laughing. It was the bright laughter that hadn't been heard from him for years. Emma wet down the compost with the yellow watering can.

This is my family, Robert thought. *This is my garden.*

There was a continuous buzzing of bumblebees and flies. Robert felt like humming, but he was afraid of drowning out the murmur of life that was rising all around him.

The next day Emma, with a gleam in her eye, shared an idea with him: "I have the solution for your petunias. We'll mix in some columbine."

The overalls she had on were too large for her. One strap

had slid down from her bare shoulder. As Robert finished uprooting the ivy, Emma came over to him.

He had a strong urge to undress her, but Cathy, recently returned from her latest runaway episode, was in her room, listening to some deafening rock music and hopping around in front of her window. There was a chance she could see them.

"I could get some that are already in bloom," Emma said.

"I don't like that idea. Their scents are going to get mixed up."

"That's the point."

"I told you I didn't want intrusive fragrances. I'd rather replace the petunias with—"

"Columbine isn't intrusive. It has a fresh, subtle scent."

"You've smelled it?"

"Nikos has some lovely columbines."

"Who's he?"

"Nikos. His shop's across the street from where I work."

The name meant nothing to him.

"He's a *florist*," she said, emphasizing the word.

Robert looked at her. "I've never seen the guy."

"He's got excellent taste," Emma assured him.

"I don't see what taste has to do with it."

She made a little rebellious face. "You can trust him. He's good at what he does."

"Why should I trust him?" Robert grumbled, his eyes on the ivy. "I've never seen this guy in my life."

He gave in on the columbine front. Emma wanted columbine, and the garden was, after all, their joint undertaking. But those columbine plants annoyed him. With them, his conception of a healing garden was shattered. Emma's fondness for aromatic plants that smelled of sophistication and luxury carried all before it.

No more sage, fennel, angelica, or verbena, the herbs to which he'd wanted to consecrate his acre of land. Emma banished them with a declaration; she said they made the yard smell like a hospital.

"A hospital?"

"Some sterile place," she replied, shears in hand. "I want a garden, not an old-folks home."

Robert protested: "I agreed to the white roses, and now they're the only things you can smell."

"Of course. That's the dominant note."

"We never talked about any dominant note."

"All gardens have one."

"But not mine! Mine's supposed to be soothing!"

"*Yours? Yours?*" she said, throwing away her shears. "I thought we were sharing this garden!"

With her cheeks aflame and her shoulders hunched, she went back inside the house.

She passed within a few inches of Robert, but he couldn't distinguish her scent.

A promiscuous jumble of fragrances prevented him.

He'd restrained himself from mentioning the florist. But that man—the Greek, as Robert called him—was no stranger to their quarrels.

Nikos Kalifatides (Robert had made inquiries) weighed heavily on his mind. And what was worse, he was infringing on his flower beds.

Nikos had supplied the seeds, the fertilizer, and the watering advice that had fomented many an argument between Emma and Robert.

Sitting by the window of a coffee shop, Robert paged through a newspaper with one eye on the building where his wife worked. The Greek's shop (NIKOS—FLOWERS AND NATURE) was also on this side of the avenue. The lettering of his sign was heavily embellished with flourishes.

" 'Flowers and Nature,' " Robert grumbled aloud. "What do you think you are, an herbalist?"

At ten minutes past five o'clock, when Emma still hadn't come out, he ordered another cappuccino. He was waiting to be served when he saw her, accompanied by a colleague. The two women were laughing, as though about a confidence they'd just exchanged.

They crossed the avenue and headed straight for the coffee shop. This was so unexpected that Robert remained at the counter, paralyzed by surprise.

Emma came in first. "What are you doing here?" she said.

She hesitated to smile.

"I came looking for you—"

"Cappuccino latte, mocha, *latte mocha*!" the barman shouted, pushing a cardboard cup toward him.

"Is something wrong? The children?"

Robert shook his head vigorously. Reassured, Emma turned to her colleague. "My husband," she said.

"I see."

She looked as sorry as Emma did.

His wife must have guessed that he suspected her of having an affair. Nevertheless, she made no effort to set his mind at rest. She even came home from work later and later.

Robert wanted to be clear about what was going on. He decided to pay a visit to the Greek.

The man lived a few minutes from their house. To give himself courage, Robert made a detour to his usual bar. Gus, the owner, received him with that mixture of embarrassment and cordiality barmen reserve for the heaviest drinkers.

"I'm on the wagon," Robert announced, taking a stool at the bar.

Gus was adjusting the sound system, lowering the volume. He nodded.

"I'm devoting myself completely to my garden."

"So what'll it be?"

For the space of an instant, Robert had the feeling he'd never replanted his garden and all that activity had existed solely in his imagination. He was a penniless writer who cheated on his wife and had shown up in this bar to drown his shame.

"Bourbon," he said, laying his hands on the bar.

He was staring at his spread fingers, but out of the corner of his eye, he could see Gus's hairy hands go into motion. A glass of liquor landed under his chin.

He took a swig and put the glass down again. It was nearly empty. The other customers—a mustached man in a sleeveless undershirt, a buxom redhead, and a puny old man Robert had never seen before—darted questioning looks at the barman. They took Robert for an eccentric or a wino.

He waited until Gus's eyes came back to his and then said, "I have a garden now. A garden and a family. I have no intention of leaving them to someone else."

"You're right," Gus said, putting up the bottle of bourbon.

"Yeah!" the old man spluttered.

"You gotta stand up for yourself, handsome," the redheaded woman said.

Robert thought he recognized her as a former actress who had always appeared in supporting roles. The two of them, the redhead and the old man, were drunk. Their half-closed eyes gleamed. Why were they laughing at something that wasn't funny? He threw some coins on the bar and left.

When he reached the Greek's house, he checked the address. Yes, he'd come to the right place. On a copper placard, letters in the same style as those he'd seen on Nikos's shop sign spelled out a single name: CHARMANCE.

It was hot. The buzzing of insects grew louder and louder. Robert began to tremble. He was burning to see the guy come out of his house. Would he be able to refrain from hitting him?

" 'Charmance,' " he muttered, as though it were a swearword. Robert hated neologisms, seeing in them only contempt for good usage. And he added that word to the list of his grievances against the Greek.

The house was either old or fixed up to seem so and decorated with rustic accessories. A few little granite fountains, some wooden barrels painted with green varnish, and several black-lacquered buckets were set out on the terrace. A horseshoe adorned the front door. The shutters were open, but the house seemed empty. Robert's gaze fell on a cart with no wheels but fitted with a handle and paddles, most probably an old machine for beating laundry. The Greek was using it as a flower planter. Robert recognized the columbine that Emma had introduced into the garden.

A walkway ran along the right side of the house. He clenched his fists and started down the walkway.

He could already imagine the blood reddening the gravel and the Greek's body dragged under the plow that stood next to the path.

Behind the house Robert found the garden. He stared at it openmouthed. The Greek's garden was three times the size of his.

The profusion of petals and stems, the alternation of greens and blues, violets and yellows, formed figures like those of an agile skater. Here and there, broad, flat areas of lawn reposed the eye. A water-lily basin made a crystalline, murmuring sound. Behind some brightly spotted orchids, Robert spotted a ginkgo tree, the kind he dreamed of possessing. It exhaled a pollen that combined each flower, each stamen, each pistil. And for the first time, Robert felt the inner peace, the sensation of harmony that his own garden, despite all the work he'd put into it, had never inspired in him.

"Naturally," he said aloud. "You're a florist. That's how you earn your living. You're a real pro."

And he began to weep.

He contemplated the Greek's garden, but it was his own ruin he was looking at. It was the futility of his efforts.

Robert noticed a small shed on his left, not far away. It contained tools, bags of fertilizer, and some clay pots. The shed adjoined a greenhouse with tinted glass panes like those in stained-glass windows. On a panel in the back of the greenhouse, there was a painting of a woman. She was wearing a blouse with an open collar and gazing at him. Robert told himself she looked like Emma, but it was hard to see at that distance.

He didn't go closer to check. He knew that whatever he did, devastating thoughts would torment him.

The florist, as it turned out, was nowhere to be found. Tears ran down Robert's cheeks, but he knew the Greek's absence was beyond his control. There was nobody for him to hit, no rival to eliminate. No way out. He'd reached the end of himself.

He wiped away his tears, retraced his steps, and after banging into the laundry contraption, got out of there fast.

As she was going home from work, Emma had a bad premonition. There wasn't a lot of traffic on the highway, but the drive seemed longer to her than usual. Robert worried her. Ever since he'd dedicated himself to gardening, he hadn't been the same. His obsession with medicinal plants indicated—she was certain of it—that some grave malady was afflicting her husband.

Why had he stopped writing? Did he want to be a horticulturist? The idea made her giggle and inadvertently sound her horn. She gripped the steering wheel and went on thinking. Even if he busted his butt for years on end, Robert would never be a patch on . . .

Her thoughts turned to him. She regretted having allowed him to paint her portrait in the greenhouse. If by some awful chance Robert ever came across that painting, she refused to answer for the consequences. She'd told Nikos so. "You don't know Robert," she'd said. "You'd best keep a rifle within reach." Nikos replied that he owned almost as many guns as flowers. Emma had shivered when she heard that.

She pressed down on the accelerator. No, this Nikos, he hadn't been a very good idea. She'd gone too far. And then there were the kids, Cathy and Victor. Would they forgive their mother if she told them the whole story?

For the first time, Emma glimpsed what had pushed her husband toward drink. Delight and remorse. Guilt. She felt full of understanding for him. But fear of the irreparable continued to torment her.

She parked in the driveway and rushed to the house. For a moment, she thought she had the wrong keys. Had he swapped them? Had he had the locks changed? These hypotheses vigorously exercised her mind before she finally managed to turn the key.

A pair of overturned sneakers—Robert's—lay on the carpet in the hallway. She ran to the living room, calling out for Cathy and Victor. Why them? Why didn't she call Robert? He was the one she was worried about. Robert, the children, the house . . . they were all part of a single whole. She'd never felt that so strongly.

Cathy and Victor stood at the sliding glass door with their backs to her. The two of them were staring out into the garden.

She couldn't see what they were looking at.

Cathy shifted her eyes toward her mother and said, "What's got into him? Why is he doing that?"

Emma went closer, put a hand on her son's shoulder, and looked out.

There was no more garden. The soil had been turned over. In the entire yard, nothing green remained.

What she saw was a coarse and dismal expanse, marked here and there by earthen mounds. Under those mounds, the roses, the columbine, and the petunias lay buried. The medicinal plants hadn't been spared, either. Petals were strewn on the ground, but all flowers had disappeared. It was as though a mole, a hundred moles, had gone wholeheartedly to work, had dug their burrows under the roots and made so many openings in the soil that every growing thing had been swallowed up.

Now it was a field of compost, and you could inhale, along with the earthy smell, the potpourri of efforts Robert and Emma had made to replant their garden.

In the midst of the disaster, there he was, on his knees. He wasn't wearing his overalls, just an undershirt and a pair of boxer shorts. His sweaty body was spattered with earth. No shovel or spade or any other tool could be seen near him. He'd turned over the soil in the yard with his bare hands.

He was staring wide-eyed into space; he seemed to be elsewhere.

Emma turned to Cathy and Victor and figured it was too

late. They'd seen the spectacle of their father pulling up and demolishing what he'd planted. Cathy had tears in her eyes. A vague smile was playing on Victor's lips.

Emma opened the sliding door and hurried over to Robert. She knelt down, removed a clod of dirt that fell on her thighs, and placed her hands on her husband's shoulders.

Robert sniffed a dense, sweet fragrance that drew him out of his torpor. He didn't hear what was being said, but it was his wife's voice. It was Emma's voice, beyond any doubt. And he was conscious of being solidly planted with her, with Emma and their children, planted together in the same compost, moved by the same shocks and the same quakes, like some of the very tenacious roots he could see around him but had been unable to pull up.

DOUGLAS

...like some of the very tenacious roots...mmm... mmm...unable to pull up.
All right. Attack.

*

If Raymond hadn't existed, I would have invented him. He's had all the experiences I missed out on. Never had the time. Never had the temptation, or the bad luck. There are so many lives out there. So many opportunities to suffer. I've always had . . . It's funny. I've always had the feeling I wasn't made for suffering. I imagined I could exempt myself from that. Even as far back as when I was in school, I didn't think collective punishments concerned me. The whole class would get an F in something, and I'd look at the others and think, "Poor mutts, they're really in for it now." I'd be surprised to see that grade on my report card too. In my case, it was a mistake.

And I always found a way of canceling the F, of coming out unscathed.

Raymond: a compost of experiences I haven't lived through.

"Compost." Sounds a lot better than "Petunias."

If I'd known suffering, if I hadn't exempted myself from it by becoming one of the three editors who count in this town, I would have been a writer like Raymond. Maybe even better than Raymond.

His life, the giant screw-up he's made of it—the two kids by the age of twenty, the debts, the booze, the wife who loves him and weighs him down, the domestic drama of the working-class guy who stubbornly keeps on writing—that's what I was looking for. The chronicle of an absurd ambition. Prometheus chained to the corner mini-mart. That's me, that's you, if we hadn't had a choice.

Raymond and I talk on the phone and write to each other. Since I started publishing his short stories, he calls me his friend, he calls me his brother. I know as much about Marianne as I would if we lived together. Sometimes I wish she would just fuck off. Take care of the kids and let me write. It's come to this. I have to pinch myself to remind me that he's the one who lives with her.

I feel empathy. My scissors aren't for cutting so deep that what's left is unrecognizable. Their work is to make the resemblance total. I look in the mirror, and who is it I see? Him or me?

*

I don't like the Greek. I don't like Nikos Kalifatides—a carnival name if I ever heard one. Raymond has too much imagination, it harms his stories. And then alcohol gives him a kind of sludgy melancholy. It's a style, yes, I see that. But the problem is it already exists. When it comes to whining short-story writers, there's a whole clan of them. Give me . . . I could name twenty.

But the most serious problem is that Raymond believes in the happy ending. "No happy ending, no sudden fall, no reprise of the opening motif." I tell my students that again and again. "Your stories must have the metabolism of an electric pencil sharpener." If they don't, the result is . . .

"Petunias." Five thousand words to say a very simple thing. "We can't eradicate our faults any more than we can the roots that bind us together. This is our garden, this is our compost."

Why use more words?

And now to clear away some brush.

RAYMOND |

No, I'm not narrow-minded. I don't see anything narrow-minded about my reaction. Douglas, I'd very much like . . . I'd very much like to understand how a short story entitled "Petunias," fifteen pages long, becomes a fragment called "Compost." Yes, a fragment! I know what a fragment looks like. Two and a half pages is a fragment.

And where's the Greek? What happened to him? I'm talking about Nikos. Nikos Kalifatides. "No one has a name like that"? Yeah, I can think of someone. The garage mechanic in my hometown. "That doesn't matter"? All right, fine. Except Nikos matters to me. "Petunias" matters to me.

And I don't recognize Robert. No, I didn't say "myself." Robert has nothing to do with me. I've never gardened in my life.

Look, I've got nothing against a little pruning, some touching up here and there. And you know how to do that, there's no doubt you know how to do that . . . but two and a half pages, that's going too far!

Mm-hmm. No, I haven't showed it to Marianne. I just opened the package a few minutes ago. I took a quick look at it. I didn't have to read it all to recognize the damage.

Huh? Oh yes, yes, I got it. No, thank *you*. I figured that was a lost cause, getting a writing grant. Taxable, but all the same . . . It's thanks to you, to your letter of recommendation. No, you wrote *that*? "A writer of the stature of . . ." They swear by him, you knew that, didn't you? And to think, I just hate his flowery style . . .

Back to "Petunias." "Comp . . ." "Petu . . ." I don't agree with you.

"Who wants to read five thousand words about gardening?" But it's more than that! It opens slowly, like a . . . The end is like a . . . a renewal for them.

"Compost" talks about love. "Petunias," I mean.

You moved it back to the fall? It doesn't take place in springtime anymore? In autumn, but you don't point it out? "Everything happens implicitly," you say? I suppose so, when you cut four thousand five hundred words! Don't give me that, Douglas. I know your Hemingway spiel by heart. *You could omit anything if you knew that you omitted and the omitted part would strengthen the story and make people feel something more than they understood.* I know that by heart. It's not an excuse. It doesn't justify your cuts.

I disagree.

A collection? You're thinking about . . . How many stories? Between fifteen and twenty? Who'll publish it? A small publisher. Your own imprint. Terrific. Your name in big letters. You negotiated for that? Of course I'm game. What do you think? My own collection . . .

About the story . . .

To summarize, if we reduce it to . . . If I keep your cuts and approve the ending . . . The story will . . .

Listen, Douglas. Listen to me, please. That story . . . it won't be mine anymore. Do you understand?

What do you mean, what story are we talking about?

RAYMOND AND MARIANNE

" 'You sign the short story, I sign the magazine. It's one inside the other, Raymond. One inside the other.' "

"He said that?"

"Word for word."

" 'One inside the other.' What does that mean?"

"He sees the climax of the story as a happy ending. That's a problem for him."

"But it's not your problem."

"According to him, the 'fictional continuity,' the . . . the 'sequencing of the narrative'—I can't remember the exact formula he used, but in any case, that aspect of a story necessarily falls within the editor's domain. That's what he said."

"And you understood him?"

"No."

"So what are you going to do?"

". . ."

"Give me 'Petunias.'"

"'Compost.'"

"Give me 'Compost.'"

"Wait till I read it."

"Raymond . . . where are you going?"

"The kitchen. I can't read my story in the bathroom."

"It's not your story, it's whatever he made out of it."

"Did I tell you he's going to put them all together? In a collection?"

"What?"

"He announced that, as casual as could be."

"He's really too much . . ."

"I'm lucky to have him. First the grant, and now a collection."

"You could have gotten the grant without his help."

"I don't think so. I'd still be trying to—"

"We can manage very well without him."

". . . to place my stories in little magazines."

"That's better than . . ."

"Than what? *Than what?* You want Sarah and Leo to think it was all for nothing? The debts, the doing without, the house that got taken from us? Our house was taken from us!"

"I know that. I know it better than anyone."

"For God's sake, Marianne. You're a teacher *and* a waitress. You bust your butt day and night because we need your tips."

"You think that doesn't bother me?"

"Then what are we talking about? Why are we fighting?"

"We're not fighting. We're talking about your stories. They're the reason why we—"

"*Our* stories."

"That's what I'm saying. If you surrender to Douglas—"

"But I'm not surrendering anything!"

"If you accept his cuts, if the stories . . . Even if they seem better after he's through with them, you'll regret it. One day you'll regret it."

"Where did I put 'Petunias'?"

"Listen. Listen to me. Stop pacing around like that. Even if the collection's a success, you're going to feel you've failed. Because you'll know you gave in to him. You'll know you took the best you had and surrendered it to Douglas."

"No."

"No?"

"I see things differently."

"Differently how?"

"I'm going to succeed *because* I gave in to him."

". . ."

"I see beyond his cuts, Marianne. Well beyond them."

"You do?"

"And you'll benefit, too. You'll have your share of . . . of the success."

"Make a note of it, then."

"Do what?"

"Write it down in a notebook."

"Of course . . ."

"I'll have my share."

"You haven't seen 'Petunias'?"

"Make a note of it."

RAYMOND

It's the tale of a guy who wants to be forgiven.

That's my subject. I'm not going to call it "Compost."

The story's full of hope. Like everything I write. Hope isn't to be found on every page, but you *do* find the possibility that . . . in the course of the . . . when you get to the end . . .

Happy endings are out of fashion, but hope remains. It's the hardest thing to grasp.

MARIANNE

I was fourteen when I met him.

I was making pocket money by selling doughnuts. It was in a convenience store outside of town. Raymond's mother worked the counter. Ray made deliveries. We said hello and good-bye to each other. One day he asked me if I felt like seeing King Solomon's mines. I was dying to shuck my apron and run off with him, but after a few seconds I said, "My parents would never let me go on such a long trip."

He frowned and then after a few moments smiled. "It's a movie," he said. "It's just a movie. It's playing real close to here."

"Ah. In that case . . ." I said, and then I went silent.

"Is that a yes?" he asked me, frowning again. I nodded.

In the very instant when he smiled at me in front of the doughnut stand, I knew I was going to marry him. Crazy, huh?

The movie was good. We went back to see it because we started kissing and missed the end. In fact, we went back several times. We tried not to kiss during the last fifteen minutes, but it was stronger than we were. Raymond wound up going to see it by himself. "I need to know how it ends," he told me, frowning. I was hurt, but I didn't insist. Sometimes you have to know when to give way. At the time, "sexism" didn't exist. We just said, "You have to know when to give way."

I gladly gave way to him because he was different. The other boys were con artists. Not him. Except for the time he made me believe he knew how to dance.

In those days, when I was almost fifteen, I read a novel about a hypnotist. He controls a young girl and makes her what he wants her to be. *Svengali*—that was his name.

Douglas is a Svengali.

The first time I talked to him on the telephone, I made a mistake: I thanked him. I said, "Thanks for buying Ray's stories and publishing them in your magazine."

"Each of us can help him," the voice in the receiver said.

"What do you mean?"

"I mean you."

"Me?"

"You most of all," Svengali said.

"Me?"

"You . . ." He drew out the word.

"And how can I help him?"

"By freeing him."

"Freeing him from what?"

"From familial constraints," he said. The words I thought I heard under his voice were "By freeing him from you . . ."

I hung up on him.

He called me back and said he was having trouble with his phone line. Douglas would never let anyone else cut *him*.

My husband's not going to sell himself, he's not going to compromise his integrity for a con artist like that. Raymond's on the verge of making an immense discovery about himself. If he can quit alcohol, if he can manage to stop drinking.

"Compost." Two and a half pages of con artistry. Some cunning tricks to take the reader in, hypnotize him with silences, with threats, with things unsaid. Nothing sincere, nothing real. A cold wind blows through it from beginning to end.

Raymond read "Compost." He couldn't get over it. I'd never seen him in such a state. He felt like he'd been swindled, cheated of his story. Our story—all he ever writes about is us.

He read those two and a half pages twenty times over.

The living-room carpet is strewn with empty beer bottles. Ray's stamping on the pages, blackening them under the soles of his shoes. The children wake up, come downstairs, and enter the living room. They look at their father, who pays them no mind. Raymond's shouting, "What does that mean, *one inside the other*?" He snatches up the pages and rips them to shreds. "It doesn't mean anything! All it means is I'm get-ting fucked!" I put my hand on my son's shoulder.

I don't think Svengali stands a chance.

DOUGLAS AND RAYMOND

"I'm sorry, Raymond. I'm terribly sorry . . . I thought you didn't want to talk to me anymore . . . I had no way of knowing . . ."

"It's my fault, Douglas. I should have called you."

". . . that you'd had a relapse."

"I'm better. I just spent three weeks in a dry-out clinic, and I'm better."

"You have to give up alcohol for good, Ray. It's the writer's poison."

" . . ."

"Liquor killed your father, didn't it?"

"It was a work accident in a sawmill. His drinking just precipitated things."

"But you're different. You don't want to precipitate any-thing."

"I was proud of him. Right to the end."

"You don't want to die at the age of fifty, do you? Listen, I've got some good news."

"You're backing down?"

"You're not going to eat your chestnut puree?"

"You can have it."

"I'll finish it for you."

"You're backing down about my stories?"

"Moving forward, you mean. I always go forward, that's how I am."

"You want to keep 'Compost' as it is?"

"No, I cut the scene in the bar. It was too much. Say, check out the little blonde."

"I thought I told you . . . Douglas. I don't want you changing my titles or the names of my characters. I don't want you chopping up my stories anymore."

"'Chopping'? Editors aren't woodcutters, Ray. Check out that little blonde—"

"Douglas!"

"You splashed my jacket."

"Sorry."

"*Chestnut Puree on Linen Jacket.*"

"I'm very sorry."

"Sounds better than the crappy paintings in the office . . . Thanks, honey. My friend's got the shakes. Has anyone ever told you you look like Sissy Spacek?"

"Douglas. I want my short stories to be published as I wrote them. Unchanged. Even if you find them too explicit."

"I think they aren't explicit enough."

"You do?"

"You believe you're telling one story. In fact, you're telling ten at the same time. It must be the alcohol that does that."

"What if that's what I'm describing? The effects of alcohol?"

"You have something to say but too many words to say it with. That's where I come in."

"Why don't you write your own short stories? Instead of cutting other people's."

"I know where my talent lies."

"In vampirism."

"You've been drinking, Ray. You wouldn't say that if you were sober."

"I *am* sober."

"But you lack humility. Did Marianne put you up to this?"

"I haven't seen her for ten days. She . . . she's left the house . . . What's in that envelope?"

"The contract for your collection . . . Can't you say anything? Well, I need your signature. When's Marianne coming back? Well? Why are you crying? Why cry when I'm giving you a contract? Be happy, Ray. Be happy and sign it with me."

MARIANNE

We used to play a game when we were around twenty or so. We'd write down bits of movie dialogue, learn them by heart, and amuse ourselves by performing the roles.

It's night. Ray's borrowed his father's van. The radio's tuned to a jazz station. I'm in the passenger seat. I recite from memory: "'I happen to love my husband. Perhaps that's an emotion you are incapable of understanding.'"

Ray puts on his grouchy voice and says, "'Perhaps.'"

"'Perhaps you've never known a woman truly in love,'" I say, like Deborah Kerr.

"'Perhaps!'" Ray growls between his teeth. "'But I have

known people to make elaborate sacrifices for reasons they themselves don't quite understand.'"

"I adore that line," I say, taking the notebook from him. "Shall we switch? That way I can say it."

"Huh?"

"We'll swap roles. I'll be Stewart Granger. 'Perhaps,'" I say, clenching my teeth. "'But I have known people to make elaborate sacrifices for reasons they themselves don't quite understand . . .' What are you doing?"

Ray turns up the volume on the radio. A trombone solo invades the interior of the van. "I don't feel like playing anymore," he replies.

I close the notebook and look out through the windshield. There's an illuminated billboard farther down the road. My eyes are too wet to read the slogan.

I give him back the notebook. After all, he's right. The actress in the family isn't me, it's my sister.

RAYMOND

September 8

Dear Douglas,
You'd laugh in my face if I told you the name of the godforsaken backwater I'm writing you from. What a hole. If it weren't for the copy of the collection you sent me—my daughter forwarded it to my address here in nowheresville, and I'm not even going to tell you where that is—yes, if it weren't for this book, a thing of my own

that I can hold in my hands, I wouldn't just be stuck in this hole, I'd be hanging from a rope in my shabby room, which features a view of the parking lot.

But the book's here. My book.

I've published thirty-five short stories in about a dozen different magazines, but strangely enough, a stack of magazines has never provided me with the sensation I feel today when I look at this collection. The sensation of having accomplished something.

I don't know how to say it any other way. Maybe it's because of the emptiness I've been surrounded by. My house is currently empty. I'm here. Marianne's gone to live with her sister. Leo stays with his grandmother. Sarah stops by the house from time to time to pick up her mail. My daughter's living with a moron I suspect of sniffing glue. I don't know what it can be that makes the guy so glassy-eyed. TV, probably. Whenever I imagine my empty house, I see the TV screen—Sarah leaves the television on to discourage thieves. Just the picture, no sound. It's a game show, one of those with a big turning wheel, and when the arrow stops on the jackpot, you can't hear the bell ring or the audience applaud. I imagine I'm watching that game show.

Ten years of my life are in this book. Seeing it published makes me feel I've won the jackpot. Thanks for the money, by the way— I'm going to be able to get my car fixed. And I should still have enough left to pay the rent on this room. The arrow stopped on the winning number, but I don't hear anything in my empty house.

Tears come to my eyes as I write. If you saw me, you'd say, "Be proud, Ray. Be content." I am, I assure you I am.

Insofar as alcohol is concerned, things are much better. God, that's bad writing: "Insofar as alcohol . . ." I should take more care with letters, now that my prose, thanks to you, is liable to become immortal . . . But I don't have the heart to make up pretty phrases. Except for this story collection of mine, everything I write seems so lame. Every hour I swallow half a glass of whiskey. That's the first step in the drying-out process. Tomorrow it will be every two hours, and so on from day to day. I've learned a cure in this center: bourbon in small doses and at fixed times. If anyone had told me I'd be boozing by the clock in here, I would never have checked in—the thought of doing things under constraint has always horrified me.

I would have liked to write to you in detail about the cuts. To discuss this one or that one. But the state I'm in doesn't allow me to concentrate for very long. Besides, there would be too much to write. My big hope right now is to recover in time to start the job you scared up for me, my first teaching job. Classes begin in a week.

I don't know if writing can be learned. I've always thought the best way was simply to get down to it, as with fishing or wood-chopping. The only valuable advice I've retained from all the workshops I've been in is "No tricks, no ruses, write with sincerity." Maybe I'll tell my students that.

Back to your cuts. Thank you, Douglas, thank you for all the sweat you put into revising my texts. I have a few reservations, of course, but as I wrote you from the hospital, you were fully authorized to muck around with the stories I submitted. (I believe that's in the contract I signed, but I don't have it in front of me.) I would have preferred to see "Petunias" instead of "Muck"—pardon me, "Compost"—I'm modifying titles too! And I would have liked to keep what passes between Robert and his wife at the beginning of the story. I find your cuts in "Compartment" a bit extreme. I don't have anything to say about "Cookie" or "Collision," even though "Collision" seemed longer when you published it in the magazine. To tell the truth, I didn't think you'd go through the stories you cut before and cut them again. I would have wanted to spare you that labor, but I understand you have to deal with the most pressing matters first. (That's something I've noticed about editors; everything goes very very slowly in the beginning and, in an equally inexplicable way, very very fast thereafter.) On a related subject, I'm enclosing a check in this envelope to cover the expenses you incurred while making your cuts. I know it cost you an arm and a leg to have all the versions of my stories typed, and I insist on being fair.

It's time for me to get re-plastered.

And if I manage to write a story between one glass and the next, be ready to unsheathe your weapon, Douglas—because we'll be starting again soon. Me from the bottom of my hole, you from the top of your skyscraper.

We make a hell of a couple, if you ask me.

Ray

P.S. If you answer this letter in the next few days, don't send your reply to the university. I was there yesterday, and they don't know who I am. The girl who handles the mail thought I was a prowler. Write me at the address on the envelope.

DOUGLAS

I see it on your faces. It's dripping out of your mouths. It's moistening your little lips, which can't wait to give me a smile.

There's only one thing on your minds: You want to please me.

It's nauseating. Your stories nauseate me—they're so much like you. "Is that good, Mr. Douglas? Is that what you want to read? Because that's what I tried to write: a story you'd want to read . . ."

HOW SHOULD I KNOW WHAT I WANT TO READ?

If I knew, I wouldn't be an editor. I'd be the guy who decides what's going to be shown on TV—I think a computer does that. It programs for tomorrow the successes of the day before yesterday. If something worked yesterday, it puts it out again the day after tomorrow. The same way with Ithaca—Ithaca's my son. He's ten years old, he collects stickers. If you present him with one that's not in his collection, he starts to cry. Do I look like I collect stickers?

Hurry up and displease me, and maybe we'll see one another again.

MARIANNE

A bad communication between postal workers, no doubt. Our regular mailman's on leave. He alone knows that if our mailbox is as flat as a pancake, it's not because we don't want any more mail, it's because you came home loaded and rolled over it. He had experience with us, he knew what was up, and so he used to put our letters under the doormat. But his colleagues just pass us up and the mail gets here three weeks late (when Sarah goes and picks it up at the post office). That's why I didn't answer you right away. Do you believe me, Ray? That's really the only reason it's taken me so long to answer you.

I can gauge how much progress you've made. Even if you didn't tell me, I could figure it out. You're in a detox center for the eighth time in three years, not to mention various stays in the hospital. I can only repeat what I've been saying to you since you started drinking—really drinking. I think it was your twentieth birthday. Keep that in mind for the day when you stop, and we'll etch a few words onto an empty bottle: "Raymond's Alcoholism. Start date–end date." Why not stop this year, when you make thirty-seven? I'm going to say it again: If what you want is to be a second-rate writer, then keep on drinking. Forget you were supposed to be counted among the best one day. Because the pact we made was that and nothing less than that. If it was less, then all our sacrifices were pointless.

Claire and I have talked and talked—it's all we do here. Talking to my sister does me a lot of good. On the telephone, it's not the same. Here at least when she cries, I can stroke her face. Claire just has to keep plugging away and not give up. It can't be easy to be an actress in a part of the country where so many actresses are out of work and a select few are always on display. I was wondering, couldn't actresses be interchangeable, like the box-office cashiers in the movie theater where I used to sell programs? They were never the same from one week to the next—I think the boss harassed every one of them. But actresses aren't interchangeable, not the way cashiers are. Can you imagine a place where all the cashiers in the country would come looking for work? No, of course not. That's why I told Claire, "While you're waiting for your chance, you should be a cashier." But she wasn't interested. Sometimes she worries me, I'm afraid she's cracking up.

She and I have that in common: not the cracking up part, but the obstinacy, like my stubborn confidence that she's going to be successful someday, even if not as an actress. And I think about us. I can't imagine that we could fail, that you could not become a great writer.

Chekhov wasn't an alcoholic, was he? How sad that he died so young. The other day it occurred to me that you ought to write a story about Chekhov. Since you love his stories so much, you should write one about him. Well, look at me, suggesting subjects to you again, when I promised myself I'd stop.

I've made myself a lot of promises.

I wake up at night and I can't remember what happened. I don't know why our house is empty, why the mail's so slow, and why these words of mine seem to have so little power to reach you.

Why are we so far from each other when we've got so much love left?

RAYMOND

"The Sorrows of Gin." A young girl watches her parents becoming alcoholics. She gets worried, feels powerless, decides to run away. She gets as far as the train station, but her escape is thwarted at the last minute. Her father comes to pick her up.

Have you all read this story? Uh . . . no, I don't have the date in my head.

(Personally, the only date I remember is the day I turned twenty, the day when I started . . . what I started.)

What interests me—sorry, I'll speak louder. What interests me in "The Sorrows of Gin" is the change in the point of view. The end of the story is narrated through the father's consciousness, whereas we see the rest, from the beginning, through the little girl's eyes. What shall I say? This story has always left me with a feeling of . . . Cheever's a master, there's no doubt about that. But this change of lens, so to speak . . . Was he right to end his story this way? In your opinion? Yes, Miss . . .

(My God, how can a girl *be* so pretty?)

What would I have done in his place? Well . . . I'm not John Cheever. Everyone has their own way of telling a story. That's a very individual, personal matter, don't you think? For example, I wrote a short story—it's called "Petunias"—where something along the same lines happens. The reader sees the end of "Petunias" through the eyes of the wife, even though the story's about her husband. I don't know why I changed the point of view at the end, but the wife seemed the obvious choice at the moment I wrote it.

You can tell a story from as many points of view as there are characters. Don't ask yourself which is the best, let it impose itself on you. In spite of you.

Sorry?

(If she doesn't stop devouring me with those big eyes, I won't be responsible for whatever I may do.)

You'd like to read "Petunias"? Well, it's been published, but under a different title: "Compost." The thing is, though, you won't find the ending of "Petunias" in "Compost."

Why did I cut the ending? It wasn't me. How shall I put it? You're not always the writer you'd like to be. Some things . . .

(There. If I stay close to the window, just in front of her, I don't see her anymore. I can keep my cool.)

Some things escape our control.

DOUGLAS

Raymond, my friend, I sympathize.

Your letter made me howl with laughter. I can imagine the scene very clearly. You in your black sunglasses, half crocked, in front of twenty or so students, all of them raising their hands and saying, "Sir, what's the magic formula?" Ah, if they knew that the only knowledge you can transmit to them—the only thing that writers can teach—is how to ruin your life in a few easy steps. Because ruining your life is the only way to wind up alone with yourself and start to write. That's the price you have to pay, no matter what anyone says.

As for the starstruck girl in the front row, I found your description of her positively mouthwatering. You should hang your scruples in the closet and get her into your bed. Especially if what you wrote me is true and she spends the breaks between classes flirting with you.

Not to be outdone along those lines, I'm going to tell you what I did last night. I was in the big amphitheater. These days there are close to a hundred groupies in every one of my workshops. I trot out my spiel on writing and addiction, being careful to conclude with a few words on how the libido can detract from stylistic perfection. I have to keep myself from laughing out loud, because at least thirty of them are taking down what I say word for word. And this is in one of the top three universities in the country. At the end of class, the choice morsel I mentioned to you the other day—Jessica Lange with even more curves—comes up to me and whispers, "I didn't completely understand your theory of the libido. Can we discuss it over a drink?" Please note that it was already midnight. She took me to her place, amigo, and at 3 a.m. I was still there, making her climb the walls. I had to get up at 7 a.m. to go to work, but at noon we started in again. This time we both climbed the walls.

But in the office I have to restrain myself. I'm having problems with Sibyll's replacement. She went and told the boss I've been groping her. That could cost me my job, and if my wife gets wind of it, I'll be going through my fourth divorce. I find the weaker sex more and more aggressive these days. It must be the zeitgeist.

Let's get back to the main point. If I should leave here—there's an opening for a fiction editor in the publishing house across the street—I'd like it to be with your second collection of stories under my arm. To raise the bidding. As you see, our fates are intertwined. So stop fearing the worst. The critics aren't going to devour you—I work on them every day of my life. Write those goddamn stories and get it over with! No excuses this time. You tell me Marianne and the kids aren't around anymore, you've got that teaching job I found for you, and if you're too scrupulous to treat yourself to the starstruck beauty in the front row who writes like Flannery O'Connor, make a story out of that.

You can't give up on me, Ray. For seven years, I've been moving heaven and earth to get you some recognition, and I need that second story collection more than ever. And don't worry, I'll firm up your work wherever necessary.

Douglas

RAYMOND

My father was a good man.

A good man and an alcoholic. I believe his legacy to me included more alcoholism than goodness, but I keep hoping to reverse the trend.

He used to take me fishing. But now, if someone should show me a map of the region where I grew up, I wouldn't be able to say where the fish are. I wouldn't even have the slightest idea. I couldn't point out the good fishing spots to anybody.

That's my current motto. I repeat it to my students: *Nobody can do your searching for you; it's up to you to find the way.* When they hear that, they seem disappointed.

Can it be that I'm not made for teaching?

The ticking of the clock fills the room. For the last five minutes, I've been one year older. I would have liked to give up alcohol. Too bad. Maybe next time.

Marianne, if you only knew . . .

I'm sorry, I woke you up. No, I was talking to myself. You can use my glass, I'll drink straight from the bottle. Has any-one ever told you you write like Flannery O'Connor? Tender to begin with, and cruel in the end. "A Good Man Is Hard to Find" made a big impression on you, too?

A good man is hard to find, but alcohol's easy.
Alcohol and pretty girls.

MARIANNE |

If Raymond could see us now! We're totally loaded. He'd
call us a pair of drunks. Stop, Claire, stop, you're killing me.

You're such a good mimic, you've really got him down.
It's like you're the one who lived with him for twenty years
and put up with his . . . No, finish it. Finish it yourself. Okay,
we'll split the dregs. Stop. You're killing me.

I almost did it, you know. I almost went to see him. I was
going to take the car, drive all the way there, and surprise him
on his birthday.

But what would have been the point? To put the pieces
back together? We've tried that a thousand times.

I had a dream the other night. I was holding a piggy bank
in my hands. I put it up to my ear and shook it. No jingling,
not the slightest sound. I looked at the piggy bank. It had a
crack in it, such a big crack I wondered how the thing could
stay in one piece. At that moment, I realized it looked just like
our house. The one that was repossessed.

And here's how the dream ended. I pressed the piggy
bank against my ear and listened again. It was like listening
to a conch shell, that whistling sound. The buried murmur of
the ocean, coming from our completely cracked house. Then
it broke into pieces.

Suppose I took your car? I could get there by dawn. Do

you think he thinks about me? Do you think he's thinking about me right now?

RAYMOND

Me, too. I borrowed other voices, too. Hemingway's, Chekhov's . . . I took myself for a ventriloquist. And now I've turned into a puppet. My editor's puppet. He speaks through me. He swallows my words and spits them out in another form. The result is I've become very cautious. I have to start writing again, but I don't want to end up in his hands. I feel blocked. I don't dare put a single word on paper for fear he'll grab hold of it.

Why are you getting dressed? Why don't you stay?

You've got "a story to write"? That's funny. I feel as though I've lived through this scene before. With the roles reversed.

I'd rather not wind up in somebody else's fiction—I'd prefer to remain my own character.

Good thing she beat it. A little while longer and she would've drunk up all my bourbon.

MARIANNE

This is just the beginning, you know, Claire. I feel it's going to catch on, it's going to grow and spread. No, not like mold. I'm serious. Listen.

Edgar says, "We're in the avant-garde, we're pathfinders."

He repeats that all day long. People don't know what they're missing. Or rather, they feel something's missing, but they don't have the words to express what it is. That's where we come in. We invite them to connect with themselves. And eventually with other people. First with themselves, then with others. The process has to start in the body. Not in the head. Thanks to us, people learn to distrust their head. Edgar and I are writing pamphlets about this. People are reluctant in the beginning. But that reluctance is a symptom of what they're missing. We don't tell them that, of course. We make them feel this need, this necessity of connecting. The first pamphlet's free. Edgar thinks it's bound to catch on and spread.

No, that would be stupid. I have to give him some room. Raymond . . . Raymond has to reach the end of himself. If I called him every day . . . I'm not saying I don't get the urge. I'm dying to call him. Edgar says, "Why do you always have to be calling up your ex-husband?" He calls him my ex-husband.

I think Raymond can win his fight with alcohol if I don't ask him how it's going every blessed day. That's between him and his conscience. It's his battle, not mine. If there weren't three hundred miles between Raymond and me, if I hadn't found a position here and he hadn't gotten that college teaching job, we would have put that much distance between ourselves anyway. To have a better chance of finding each other again.

Yesterday Edgar suggested we go away for the weekend. I pointed out that I was wearing a wedding ring, and that it means something. Edgar said he knew of wedding rings whose only function was to prevent their owners from connecting with anyone else. Sometimes he lays it on a bit thick.

Do you know that Raymond's practically a celebrity? His story collection has received rave reviews, there's been a ton of articles written about him, and invitations have come pouring in from all over the country. People want to meet him. Critics say he writes about the losers and rejects of society like nobody else. I should find that delightful. Except that the losers are us. They're me. And I'm supposed to be delighted about that? Thanks for the compliment! I'd just as soon not be in his stories.

I feel more peaceful today. Thanks to you, Claire, and the time I spent with you.

When I lose hope, I reassure myself by remembering that Raymond's right on the verge of making a huge discovery about himself. Nobody else can make it for him.

And when he does, he'll come back.

Then we'll be together again.

RAYMOND AND JOANNE

It's springtime. I ought to find all this delightful—the mild weather, the starry night, the festive atmosphere pervading this house.

There's a certain fervor in the air.

The house belongs to a specialist in religious history. I'm not sure whether the host is a man or a woman. I heard someone say "professor," but I didn't catch the name. Makes no difference; I'm supposed to enjoy myself. To have a delightful time, like everybody else.

The jazz record that's been playing since I got here makes

me feel like tapping my feet. Someone says, "I always feel more creative when swing music's in the air." We're on a university campus, no doubt about that.

Professors and students are laughing together, barriers are falling, and I'm staying far away from the ginger punch they're ladling out in the back room.

For the past three weeks, I've been limiting myself to one drink a day. Not a single drop more. I can smell the rum in that punch from here, and its vapors make me tremble, I hope imperceptibly. If I let myself go, if I have so much as a taste, I'll be finished. I'll be dead.

Fortunately there's a rumor going around: "The ginger punch is vile. Avoid it." That suits me fine. I'll stick with water.

I smile at anyone who smiles at me, but I'm not budging an inch. I feign interest in the host's library, whoever he or she may be. Bibles in every language, dating from every time period. The titles of the books not in the Bible section all seem to contain the word *Religion*, or in some cases *Faith*. I still haven't decided which of the two I prefer when I notice a couple of others: *Belief* and *Dogma*. It occurs to me that a subject with so many different designations must be a highly problematic subject indeed. I congratulate myself on being a writer of few words.

I look for a place to put my paper cup so I can leaf through a book about crucifixion.

At that moment, a woman with long black tresses and a seashell hair clip plants herself in front of me. She's my age. Her incisors point in several directions, which gives her a certain charm. Her eyelids are half closed; her lips ripple and twitch. She looks like she's teetering on the edge of a laughing fit.

As I'm considering the seashell, I hear her say, "All right, on a scale from one to ten, how much do you think you're going to like it?"

I lower my eyes and see that she's handing me a cup of punch.

"No thanks. I'm sticking with water."

Her lips form an O. "What rotten luck. Everyone here is sticking with water. Or Scotch."

I smile.

"Try it all the same."

She holds out the cup. The punch has a brackish color.

"Sorry, but I recently stopped drinking."

Her eyes brighten. I apparently interest her.

"Both of my ex-husbands were alcoholics."

"My goodness, you're dangerous!"

She looks at me as if she doesn't understand and then holds out the cup again. "Oh, come on, there's hardly any alcohol in it. Nobody wants any." (She looks sidelong at the other guests.) "I'm starting to believe this is some kind of practical joke."

"If it is, nobody told me about it."

To see her smile again, I take the cup. But I don't lift it to my mouth.

Her face lights up. "Well then, on a scale from one to ten, how much do you think you're going to like it?"

"Why are you asking me that?"

"Anticipation increases pleasure."

"Anticipation?"

"Increases pleasure," she repeats.

I raise my eyebrows.

She says, "First rule of psychomarketing."

"Is that your specialty?"

"No, it's just a day job. I'm actually a poetess. People make fun of me when I say that. But not you, strangely enough."

"And what's the second rule?"

"Sorry?"

"Of psychomarketing."

"Uhh . . . it seems to have slipped my mind. As I said, it's just a day job. I spend three hours a day in a huge supermarket. I get customers to try a range of products. Before they do, I ask them—you always have to ask them *before*—"

"Before what?"

"Before they taste whatever it is. I offer them paprika chips or sausage slices or cubes of Gorgonzola or—"

"Okay, I get it."

"And so on and so forth, and I say, how much do you think you're going to like these blah blah blah."

"And that increases their pleasure?"

"Every time. People really enjoy themselves. Or pretend to so I'll leave them alone. Don't you want some of my punch?"

"Five."

"Sorry?"

"I think I'm going to give it a five."

"That's all? You're not making much of a commitment."

I search for a good comeback but find none. Her presence agitates me.

"You don't want a taste?"

"Listen, uh . . . what's your name?"

"Joanne."

My legs start to feel wobbly.

"And yours?"

"Raymond."

"Do you teach?"

"I run a writing workshop. CW-6."

"Well, isn't that something? I run CW-7. We're neighbors."

"Our classrooms?"

"No, just the workshop numbers."

"Ah," I say, disappointed.

"And what do you write?"

"Short stories."

"You're shaking . . . Give me that cup." She takes back the punch I haven't touched.

"Are you interested in short stories?" I ask her.

"I love good stories. I read the ones my friends write and give them my opinion."

"Do they pay attention to what you say?"

"Every time. I'm an excellent . . . diagnostician," she says, swaying on her legs.

She's drunk too much punch. It must contain more alcohol than she's willing to admit. "You should wear a lab coat," I remark. "And a stethoscope."

She laughs. Her tongue protrudes slightly and makes her lips glisten. "Come on," she says. "Don't be sarcastic."

"Your poems . . . what are they like?"

She blinks as though pondering the question.

"In the beginning I wrote short pieces, haiku-type things."

I raise my eyebrows. She starts to recite: *"A stranger here and elsewhere / A screen between the world and me / Two booze-hounds for husbands."*

"Go on."

"That's all."

I ask myself how she got put in charge of the CW-7 workshop, but I find her devilishly exciting.

She opens her eyes wide. "You don't believe me, do you?"

"Uh . . ."

"You didn't think that was poetry?"

She looks ready to throw her punch in my face.

"No."

"So much the better." She starts smiling again. "Still," she goes on, "I really did write short when I started. Really *very very* short," she repeats, as if I didn't understand her. "I need to blossom out now. I need amplitude. You follow me?"

"I like amplitude."

She takes a little swallow of punch and begins to talk again, as if she's thinking out loud. "The more time passes, the more I feel I have to say. And the more space I need to say it in."

I nod my head vigorously. In a tone filled with self-assurance, I say, "Concision is for novices."

"Absolutely right. You can't express all the richness of existence in five-word sentences."

"Especially if they don't have any commas."

"Right again!"

There's a silence. I stammer, "Nevertheless . . . I know a word . . ."

I look her in the eye. I feel as though I've lived beside her for decades.

"You're still trembling. Are you cold?" Her fingers graze the back of my hand.

"No, I feel fine. I'm feeling better and better."

She takes my water glass and puts it on the table. Then she raises her cup and says, "Never fear, you can drink some."

I take a swig.

"What were you saying?"

"I was saying I know a word . . . a word that suffices by itself to express a great many things."

"What word?"

"*Mamihlapinatapei.*"

She furrows her brow.

"It comes from Tierra del Fuego."

She tries to say it: "*Mami* . . ."

". . . *hlapinatapei.*"

She tilts her head as though she's concentrating. I go on: "I think it means, 'The look two people share when both of them want something to start but neither dares to make the first move.'"

I lower my eyes. Joanne rises on the tips of her toes. Her mouth is very close to mine. We kiss.

She asks me, "On a scale from one to ten, how much do you think you're going to like it?"

I can't hear the music anymore.

"Ten," I answer. "Ten, no doubt."

There's a smell of doughnuts in the room.

I have the feeling my life's starting over. I died the first time, and now it's starting over.

DOUGLAS

"Minimalism." Don't you get it?

I'm surprised this word hasn't caught on in literary circles.

It came to me by accident. The best ideas come like that. A word thrown out without a thought. As it happens, my wife was the one who threw it out. My ex-wife, the third one—no, the fourth. Before she left, before she cleared out, she said, "I'm not putting up with this anymore, you hear me? I've never gotten used to all these books cluttering up the apartment. I've never felt at home here. What are you trying to do, Douglas, build a wall of books between us?" Those were her parting words, right before she stepped out onto the landing. Wait, there's more. Still in the doorway, she says, "When I want to walk across the living room or down the hall, I have to step over rows and rows of volumes, I have to dodge around piles of books, piles that go up to the ceiling." She makes a motion with her hands as if somebody's strangling her. And then, before she slams the door, she says, "Me, I'm a minimalist!"

Her name's Judith. She left me with that word. I really owe her a lot.

What is minimalism?

It's the crackle of a sentence, the whiplash of an astoundingly concise turn of phrase, a newborn tale that dies in your hands. *Not with a bang but a whimper.*

A muffled noise, an invisible gash, emptiness; and yet the shadow of something. There are those who have sung the praises of the shadow. I'd like to praise emptiness. Without disclosing what it conceals.

Don't ask me, it would spoil your pleasure.

I find it ironic that you've come today. My last day at the magazine. No, it's a scoop. You're the first to hear it. I'm giving it to you, along with minimalism.

At the very moment when I'm leaving the magazine, you come and ask me how things are going. You want me to appraise—how did you put it?—"the art of the short story in our country." Strike "art," strike "short story," strike "country." Call your article "The Secret Life of Our Time." That's the title of my first anthology. My stories have never been about anything else. I've been whispering my secrets for seven years. Before getting fired.

You've been here before? Really? In this office? Seven years ago . . . Well, how can you expect me to remember that? A student. Do you have any idea how many eager female students I've had? Yes, I know what that sounds like: Do you have any idea how many eager female students I've had in my bed?

The most annoying part of the whole thing is that I'm not going to be able to take my stained-glass window with me. The outfit across the street has a rule—all the windows must be the same. You see? Already I have to contend with formatting. I held out a long time, but they got me in the end. They kept adding zeros. No, I won't tell you the figure.

Of course I'm keeping my authors. Why should they leave me? I love them like my children. And as for the ones who aren't novelists, the short-story specialists, well, I'll publish them in collections.

Raymond—you know the author I mean?—when I talk about minimalism, I think of Ray. It's as if the very word was invented for him. No, I didn't ask his opinion. Be careful; writers don't like labels. The only ones they're willing to put up with are the bar codes on the backs of their books. Because nobody can decipher them. But for somebody who knows how to read between the lines, Raymond's a minimalist.

So your article, when does it come out? In the weekend supplement? On page one? Listen, I'm not going to give you his telephone number. He doesn't like to be disturbed. But you can run with minimalism, don't worry. He'll thank you. Raymond expects only one thing: to be recognized for what he is.

You can quote me if you want, but the word's in the air. Minimalism is the environment we live in. Well, if you insist on a source, attribute the word to Judith. Say it comes from a woman who's leaving and slamming the door behind her.

July, you say? Perfect. I'm publishing Raymond that same month. I can already envision it: your report on minimalism on page one, and inside a boxed article about his story collection. I could buy space and run an ad for my list. How much space do you have left?

Now I remember. You had a scarf around your neck. You didn't take it off, not even in bed. What about the scars on your throat? It's much sexier when they're visible. Look here, see my scales. Do I try to hide them?

Married already? A married woman, the mother of two children, and a literary critic. All that in seven years. I bet you read Kerouac at night. I do too, you know. I too let books live my life in place of me.

No, I have no idea what I'm going to do with that stained-glass window. Don't you know somebody who could buy it off me?

JOANNE

I didn't tell him everything when I met him. I made out I'd never seen him.

But I knew him already. I was waiting for him.

I'd watched his hands. They shook the way my former husbands' hands did. It was in a bookstore, about a year ago. He'd come there to talk about his short stories. I paged through them. Then I read them over and over. So I knew Ray well before I met him. I followed the grooves of his sentences like someone stroking a beloved face. I figured out where his pain was.

When I saw him the other night, it was like a sign. I gulped down two cups of punch and headed straight for him.

There he was, encumbered with himself. I wasn't afraid I'd make him drink, I could tell how much strength there was under his fragile exterior. My ex-husbands were different. Rough exteriors, fragility underneath. I wasn't able to heal them. They no longer believed in their luck. But Raymond . . . I tried right away to coax him into drinking. As if I was challenging him to stop the very next day.

To tell the truth, it wasn't as calculated as all that. After the fact, I can always find the reasons behind my intuitions. I spread a layer of glue over them so they'll stay put. I am, if you will, a post-sensual intellectual.

"Glue Girl." I had a boyfriend who called me that, because he thought I was full of fixations. "Glue Girl." I like that a lot. I dumped the boyfriend and kept the nickname.

To Raymond, I'm Joanne. He doesn't know what's in store for him.

Happiness without end.

DOUGLAS

June 3

Good grief, Raymond, if I'd had any idea . . . Is she really the one I'm thinking of? We're talking about the same Joanne? I'm writing because her name rings some kind of bell. Three or four years ago, a poet who was one only in her imagination sent me a package, an envelope stuffed with her verses. Well, believe it or not, I read them. On weekends I treat myself to poetry. I read Paradise Lost *twice a year, and also Dante's* Purgatory, *which is a documentary about the publishing business.*

Her verses were worthless. I hope her cooking's better than her poetry. And I hope she knows how to fix drinks. I've always thought a person needs two reasons for being with someone else. One isn't enough. Take the word of an expert, Ray: One isn't enough.

The more I read her, the more she exasperated me. A prime example of lyrical psoriasis, your Joanne. Not everyone can be Anne Sexton.

But enough talk about poetry. I've moved the publication date of your collection up three months—an opportunity appeared and I had to seize it, I'll spare you the details. I made an unimaginable spectacle of myself in the marketing department, and now those analphabets seem to be on board. For the first time, they're going to devote as many resources to promoting a collection of short stories as they do to promoting a novel. They're going to pull out all the stops. I have a meeting Monday about this.

Your book's publication date is July 20. The date when a man walked on the moon, and the date when I launch Ray into the literary cosmos.

I think you should settle into your chair. Are you good and comfortable? You know I'm waiting for your corrections, I mean your validations of mine. I'd appreciate it if you'd get busy. Don't forget I have a load of novels to take on between now and July 20. Poor me . . . Novels aren't like stories, it's a lot harder to remove their bones. When I get down to work on a novel, it turns into something like a wrecked car. Sometimes I take out the engine by mistake, sometimes I remove the chassis, and sometimes all four wheels because I think they're useless. You get the picture? Ever since I started editing novels, I feel like I live in an automobile graveyard.

Douglas

P.S. Don't be mad at me for that section about Joanne . . . If she is, as you say, "a woman from the working class, an alter ego," so much the better. You know what happens when someone tries to step out of his proper milieu. Kipling shows the consequences in his story "Beyond the Pale": The guy gets his balls cut off. Ah, Kipling, what concision. I don't know why he's considered old-fashioned.

RAYMOND

Joanne has given me two scarves. A blue one last month, to celebrate our meeting. Then, a few days ago, she signed a contract with a publishing house. Her next collection of poems will appear next fall. And to mark the event, she gave me another scarf. That one's green.

Their patterns are invisible to the naked eye. The label reads "70% cashmere, 30% silk." I told Joanne, "These are luxury gifts. They're too expensive for me." She answered, "Nothing's too expensive for you." I was surprised to hear that, but I didn't say anything.

Joanne's scarves really look good on me, although this isn't the season for them. Who wears scarves in summer? I wrap them around my neck. One one day, and the next day the other. They keep me warm. Maybe even too warm.

The idea of losing them terrifies me.

MARIANNE

He visits me without any warning. "You could have called me first," I say. He wanders around the living room and smokes all my cigarettes. When I notice the scarf around his neck, I have to laugh. Ray has never bought or worn a scarf. It's a gift from a woman, a way of marking her territory. Someone's got her hooks in him. It's serious this time. I can tell by how agitated he is.

Or is it because he's off the booze?

"I'm happy, Ray. I'm so happy you've quit drinking."

"It's not that easy. A daily struggle."

"I'm sure. Twenty years of alcoholism . . ."

"Almost as long as our marriage."

The words strike me like a slap in the face. I'm stunned for a moment.

"Did you have to say that?"

"What do you mean?"

"Did you have to make that comparison? What's your point?"

"It was just a remark, that's all."

"There are more positive things to say about our twenty years of marriage."

"What's up? Are we going to have an argument?"

"I didn't force you to come here."

"I had to come. I've got a favor to ask you."

"I'm sure you do. You wouldn't have come otherwise."

He sits down on the edge of a chair. Like a guy who's just passing through.

"How's Edgar?"

"He's fine. We're really happy."

I have a feeling I sound false. It's part of the feeling I have that whatever I say about Edgar is always going to sound false.

"Fabulous."

I'm sure he doesn't give a shit. "How about you?"

"I'm good. I quit drinking."

"I know, you just told me."

He looks at me out of the corner of his eye.

"Did you think I could do it?"

"Do what?"

"Stop. Did you think I had it in me?"

"What do you mean? What are you trying to prove?"

"Nothing at all. Nothing, for Pete's sake!"

He loosens his scarf. It looks like it's keeping him warmer than he wants. I lower my eyes to the carpet. If I look at him too long, I'm afraid I'll start to cry.

I stammer, "You have the nerve to tell me . . . You're implying I didn't believe you were capable of quitting . . . As if staying with me was what drove you to drink—"

"That's not what I said."

"Meanwhile this other woman, your Joanne—"

"Did I mention her name?"

I couldn't hold myself back. I heard the name "Joanne" by accident from some friends who thought I already knew it.

"You're covered with her name. You've got it all over you, from head to foot. All I have to do is look at you and it goes right through me."

He tries but fails to flick on his cigarette lighter. He lowers his hands and talks with the unlit cigarette in his mouth. "What's with all the dramatics? Am I the only one of us who's taken up with somebody else?"

"Yes, the only one!" I shout, praying that Edgar doesn't come home at that moment.

Raymond snatches the unlit cigarette out of his mouth. "We have to make our lives over! We both have to make new lives for ourselves!"

"Oh, just the thing," I say, gulping. "That makes me . . ." I can't talk, and I just let the tears flow.

"Marianne . . ."

I press the palms of my hands against my eyelids. "Why did you come here?"

I hear his legs bending. His joints crack. I move my hands and see him kneeling on the floor in front of me. He has literally gone down on his knees.

He kneels there without speaking. Like someone gathering his thoughts.

Several seconds pass.

"Listen, you have to stand up. I don't want Edgar to see you in that position. My husband's not a wimp."

He remains on his knees.

"Stand up!"

He acts as though he didn't hear me. He takes the hem of my skirt in his fingers and pulls me to him.

"Marianne."

I turn my eyes to the entrance hall. The front door is wide open.

I let my fingers drop to his hair.

If Edgar came in now, our relationship would be over. I could go back to Ray with no scruples whatsoever.

Yes, if he should come in right now, that would suit me fine. His jaw would fall off. His pamphlets on spirituality would be scattered over the carpet. I'd gaze at him defiantly. He wouldn't be able to remind me once again that he picked me up in pieces and glued them back together with the help of the *I Ching*.

Because Ray will always love me. Whatever Edgar may say, Ray will always love me.

He starts coughing. I come out of my reverie. A racking cough shakes his chest.

"What's wrong with you?"

"Nothing."

He stands up. I see his trembling hands.

Without a word, I go behind the bar and pour him a soda pop. The sugar in soft drinks reduces his need for alcohol. He's stopped drinking, but he'll never stop sugar. Or cigarettes, or writing stories.

I hand him the glass and the bottle.

"Do you have a new TV?" he asks, nodding.

"It's Edgar's."

"What's on this time of day?"

"Nothing. It's the elections."

He sits on the sofa, not coughing anymore.

"You want a piece of cake?"

"It seems my stories have political content."

"So no cake, then?"

"I wasn't really aware that they did, but the academics have detected it. Nothing escapes them."

I sit down across from him. "Is that a good thing?"

"What?"

"To have political content."

He furrows his brow. "That depends on what the content contains. I mean, on who's analyzing the content."

"I know what you want to ask me."

He's laid his scarf on the sofa beside him. The long piece of fabric curls across the cushions like a snake. I have a clear picture of myself chopping it in two with one blow, the way knights do in the tales of chivalry I assign my students.

"This is a waste of time," I say. "This is all a waste of time."

"What?"

"You can have it. You don't need to ask for it."

". . ."

"It's her idea, right?"

"Who are you talking about?"

"Your poet girlfriend. God, I feel stupid! She's managed to make me stupid from a distance."

I think about how much strength it's going to take to get up and drive to school tomorrow. I don't know whether I'll have that much strength.

"I'll file the petition," I say.

"Huh?"

"For our divorce."

There's a silence.

Then I hear him say, almost under his breath, "Thanks."

A sigh escapes me.

He stands up and pats his thighs. "I have to go."

A thought comes to me. I won't be in his stories anymore. He's the one who's leaving, but I'm the one who feels she's been kicked out.

"Thanks for the soda."

I watch him go away. I have no voice. I'm dispossessed. Twenty years of our life together, recycled into his writing. Stories that no longer belong to me.

I pick up the scarf and throw it into the garbage disposal.

I go back to the living room and sit on the sofa. I'm having trouble swallowing saliva. It accumulates in my mouth. I feel as though I'm entirely in my mouth, bogged down in my own saliva.

An engine starts up outside.

Edgar walks into the house.

"Marianne? Was that your husband I just saw coming out of the driveway?"

I try to gather enough strength to say, "My ex-husband."

But I can't do it. I can't pronounce that syllable, that word.

JOANNE

The night when he was supposed to come back from his wife's house, I couldn't sleep. I waited up for him.

We weren't living together yet. The sky was full of stars. I sat on the balcony. I was trying to recognize the birds by their calls.

I was afraid Raymond wouldn't come back, I was afraid he'd decide to stay there with her.

I knew he was going to ask her for a divorce. I could see it in his eyes. He and I couldn't go any farther unless he broke all ties with her. We'd told each other that, though not in so many words. His wife was present in every fiber of his body. I didn't expect to root her out utterly, but their divorce could be a start.

Three o'clock and he still wasn't back. I made a wish. Forget the divorce. Let him stay married to her, but at least let him come back. Don't let him be taken from me.

No shooting stars. Abnormal in a summer sky. But after my father's alcoholism, my brother's death, and my two divorces, everything's abnormal. Raymond came into my life like a shooting star. I tremble at the thought that I may not

see him again. After so many anomalies, not seeing him anymore would be in the order of things.

A star streaked across the night sky. I heard the rattling
of that clunker he drives.

He surged out of the darkness, grumbling: "I blew a tire
twelve miles from here. I couldn't get the jack to work, and I
had all kinds of other problems besides!"

I didn't give him time to say anything more. I flung myself
on him, and we made love.

In the morning I made him some coffee and then went to
work. Before I left, he sat down at his typewriter.

When I called him around noon, he was still typing.
In last night's exertions, he said, we'd broken my bracelet. I
looked at my wrist, and my glass bracelet was gone. I told him
it wasn't important, hung up, and left to teach a class.

Yeats. "The Circus Animals' Desertion." We could spend
weeks on this poem, don't you think?

During the class, I got distracted for a moment. Where
had I read that a broken bracelet is the sign of a widow in
India? I drove that thought out of my mind.

Look at the last line. "In the foul rag-and-bone shop of
the heart." What do you think that refers to?

The students looked puzzled and kept their lowered eyes
fixed on those words, as if they were written in a foreign language.

Not long afterward, Raymond and I moved in together.
That way there was less chance of losing each other.

DOUGLAS

Are you talking to me? Are you wiggling your curves under my nose on purpose?

Of course I know how to read. That's what I'm paid for. It says *General Expenses*. That's not one of my titles. I don't see what that's doing among my titles.

Look, these charts of yours, I don't care about them. I'm an editor, you understand? Ed-i-tor, that's my profession. You dream about titles with sales on an exponential curve. I dream about titles that reduce the level of general stupidity. I don't know whether we're going to be able to understand each other.

Raymond, yes. His new short-story collection. Of course there's a market for it. Intelligence is a vast market. Sensitivity, too. An exponential market. What did you say? You wouldn't give *that* to read it? How unfortunate. For you, I mean. You've excluded yourself from the market.

Listen, if that's what you're looking for—"a big hit with every title"—my answer is that you've got *a sure recipe for disaster*. Do you understand me? Every time you aim for a big hit, it will be a disaster.

What? You want to reduce my production? Cut back on my titles? "The majority stockholder." Who's that? I don't know him, we've never met. Let's have a look at him. Pull him out of your sleeve.

You see the building across the street? Not the top floor, the one right below it. You see that office? It's the fiction editor's office. You'll notice that it's empty. Nobody's occupying it. They can't find anyone to replace me. No, no, you'd better look again. That's not the photocopy room.

So what exactly did you do before this? Let me guess. Television? Film? What? "Soft drinks"? You used to sell soda pop and you were recruited for the publishing business? Well, then it's not your fault. It's nobody's fault.

No, don't turn down the air-conditioning, I've got an allergy. The air-conditioning won't make any difference. I have a kind of pruritus.

I've got one more minute?

I'm going to tell you what I think. A world where soda-pop salesmen are charged with promoting books is not at all reassuring. Not for me, not for my children, and not for my children's children.

That's what I think.

Less than a minute. *Brevity is the soul of wit.*

RAYMOND

"Happiness," yes. You could say that. But it's a fragile happiness. The demons could appear again at any moment.

To tell the truth, I would have relapsed without Joanne. The very thought makes me dizzy. To be aware that your happiness is hanging by a single thread, that it depends on just one person . . . I'd rather not think about it. And then there's the thread I spin day after day, writing and staying sober and avoiding retrospection.

I'm trying to hang in there. In the morning, when I look down at the eggs on my plate and it seems they're about to jump at my face, when everything's quivering and I think the milk bottle's a quart of vodka, I tell myself I'm screwed, I'm going to relapse, it's only been a year and my reprieve is over.

A year's not much, but in a year my life has come back, as though returned to its proper place. All I had to do is fall in love with a lady poet to whom you once sent one of those scathing letters you're so uniquely good at. Joanne kept your letter as a souvenir. She showed it to me. Let's disregard the passage where you say she's "Sylvia Plath as barfly" and the other one where you call her a "soap-opera Elizabeth Bishop." Let's disregard all that. I want you to know that Joanne's ready to smoke the peace pipe with you. She's looking over your cuts, and she's far from finding all of them bad. Some, but not all.

And speaking of those cuts: I got a slight chill from your last letter, from your request that I ratify your changes without even looking at them. I know you're under time pressure, but I'd like at least to glance at the manuscript before giving you the green light. Besides, it so happens that I have a new story cooking, which doesn't leave me much time for going over old ones again. So Joanne's applying herself to that task. As soon as I finish my story—it's called "The Mattress," for want of a better title—as soon as I finish it, I'll let you know and we'll finalize my collection.

What exactly do you mean when you talk about "forcing the house to publish the collection right"? I thought you had the marketing division in your pocket. But I suppose I'm getting worried about nothing. At this moment, my sky contains no cloud. Why should I try to put one in?

Raymond

JOANNE

There are prowlers in front of our house.

Not at night, but in broad daylight. They look like potential renters checking out the neighborhood. Yesterday a young couple, a boy and a girl holding hands, stopped by our mailbox. They took a picture of it. As if that rusty old thing was a museum piece.

In the end I figured it out. Those weren't prowlers, they were Raymond's readers.

His stories are doing surprisingly well. There are publishers who want to translate his work in Turkey, in Japan, in Korea. Countries whose existence we're hardly aware of. Raymond doesn't know what to think about all this, he says it won't last, he says people must be mistaking him for someone else. He's so accustomed to being pursued by creditors he can't imagine things are any different now. He's still afraid to answer the telephone.

I feel like putting up a sign: DO NOT DISTURB. WRITERS AT WORK.

Now that I'm reviewing his short-story collection, now that I'm penciling in corrections as he asked me to, I feel as though I'm cooperating in a common endeavor with him. As though I'm mingling my voice with his.

I've never felt my existence so intensely.

He rarely speaks of his ex-wife. Sometimes he complains about having to send her money. Money he doesn't have but sends her all the same. As if he felt indebted to her. He also sends checks to his children. "They're bleeding me white," he gripes. "It's their mission in life." They're both over twenty; Raymond doesn't know when it's going to stop.

"Imagine," he says. "Imagine that my collection scores a big success. Just imagine it for a moment. You know what would happen? They'd still bleed me white. Yeah, that would just give them an excuse."

He ponders that and settles down to writing again.

I don't ask him questions about his past. If I want to know more about it, I read his stories. I know they're partly invented. I know it's not really him and not really his ex-wife. But the feelings are genuine. They sound too true to be made up.

There are some feelings I'd like to cut out of Ray's stories. Traces of love I'd like to send back into the past, into the void.

Do I have the right to do that?

Will he authorize me to do that?

The Mattress

It was around the end of May. Dan telephoned to announce that he was going to stop by our house. We hadn't spoken for months. We got news of each other from our children. They'd call up to see if we were getting back together. But from Dan there had been nothing but radio silence. I thought about him daily, and I figured I had a place in his thoughts too. In any case, I hoped so.

I was surprised to hear him say "our house" on the telephone. He didn't use those words when we lived together. He'd say "the honky-tonk," because our house was the place where people drank and partied, and also where our kids' fights would end up with one of them throwing a bedside lamp at the other one's head. A noisy, bright, disorderly place, open to our friends and our children's friends. Until someone got hurt and we'd dial 911.

Our house. Those words didn't seem to imply just Dan and me anymore.

We'd been married for more than twenty years. On the eve of our anniversary, Dan cried out, "Twenty years! Shit! You could cram a whole life into that much time."

He flipped through the calendar, as if looking for the years gone by.

"We *have* crammed a whole life into them," I replied. "We've crammed two lives into them, in case you forgot."

I was talking about Vincent and Christine. Now that they're grown up, they don't live at home anymore. Dan was afraid of being alone in the silent honky-tonk.

A few days later, he decided to leave. He was seeing a woman, I think. Or maybe he met her after he left. What difference did it make? He wasn't there anymore.

When he talked about stopping by our house, I asked him, "What do you mean, *our house*?"

He launched into a confused explanation, pausing at length between sentences. I could hear him breathing. It was as though he was standing next to me.

"I've been invited to a colloquium on my stories. I'll be in the area. We could see each other," he said. "I'd like to see you," he added.

Dan had become a celebrity since the publication of his short-story collection. I would have liked to be happy for him, but something stopped me. I'd sip my coffee and look at the kitchen table. That was where he used to sit down to work. The Formica tabletop still carried his typewriter's mark, a worn rectangle paler than the rest of the surface.

I clenched my fist on the telephone cord. There was static.

"I'd like to see you," he said again.

I sighed. The sigh came back into my ear, a sound amplified by distance.

Dan was waiting. I felt I had to respond to him.

"I won't be here. I'm going to my aunt's."

"Your aunt Susie?"

"She needs help."

Silence fell. I had the sensation that I was Christine, in the act of lying to her mother. My daughter's an adult, but I'm still always on the alert for the slightest quaver in her voice.

"I could go with you."

Dan was talking like he was sitting in the kitchen. I could picture him raising his eyes from his typewriter and inviting himself to my aunt's house.

We'd been there together three years before. Dan and Uncle Paul had stayed up late into the night, drinking and talking. We'd slept upstairs in the guest room. I could hear the sound of the sea, so close the waves seemed to be sloshing around the bed. I dreamed I was adrift on a raft.

"If you want, I'll go with you."

His voice brought me back to the present. I said, "I thought you were with . . . I mean I supposed there was—"

"Nobody, Chloe. Believe me. There's nobody around."

I didn't want to hear any more of that. After all those weeks, I still hadn't gotten used to his absence. Not for a moment. I kept hoping and praying. As hard as when I wanted him to stop drinking.

And then one day he did it. He hasn't drunk alcohol since.

"Come and we'll see."

We agreed on a date and I hung up. Before he did, I believe.

A few seconds later, I started feeling I'd been had. I'd always been an easy mark on the telephone. I'd give people my credit card number. I'd put myself in the red. Dan knew I yielded easily to temptation. He'd shake his head after seeing me hang up and then go back to his writing.

I lit a cigarette and stared at the table.

"Why did I tell you to come?"

My aunt was delighted at the prospect of our visit. She

was aware that Dan had left me. I didn't let on that we were inviting ourselves to her house. I just said we'd be passing that way and we could stop by to see her.

"Good idea," she said. "Come while there's still time. We live in the civilization of the last chance, right?"

Aunt Susie had some favorite turns of phrase. They dated from when she'd worked as the editorial secretary of a history journal. The editor in chief was an alcoholic named Walter Sage. More than once, she'd written an editorial that he was unable to finish on account of being intoxicated. The journal wound up in bankruptcy, but Aunt Susie had seemed quite happy in the days when she was writing Walter Sage's editorials, and she retained a marked interest in what she called "immediate history." When she watched the TV news, she expressed opinions her husband, forced to listen to them, was the first to hear. Sunk in a chair after his day of work, he'd give his wife perplexed looks when she declared, "There's the U.K., pulling that Trafalgar trick again," or "Something's rotten in the Dominican Republic." Who could understand what she was talking about?

She might have stayed like that for years, spending peaceful days, occasionally voicing her opinions in enigmatic form. But then life played her a dirty trick.

For the past five or six months, more or less since Dan left me, Uncle Paul had lost possession of his mental faculties. The medical diagnosis had come down like a guillotine blade. In the near future, he would stop being able to recognize his wife.

At the age of sixty, Uncle Paul, a former insurance

salesman, divided his time between his classes in business school and his consulting work. Before the first signs of his disease, his mind had been lightning-quick. But in the past few weeks he'd had to quit going to class and seeing clients.

According to my aunt, he would sit in the living room and look at the ocean. Sometimes he'd reply to his wife's questions, which she asked in an effort to revive his memory. I don't know if she continued to express her political opinions now that he was even less capable of understanding them.

Every passing day blurred the external world a bit more.

Thinking about my aunt in that big oceanfront house, imagining her with her steadily declining husband, kept me from sleeping. It's also true that I'd been having a lot of trouble sleeping ever since Dan left.

Sleeping pills had no effect. Once, after hours of tossing and turning in my bed, I went down to the kitchen, turned on the little TV set Dan had given me, and watched one of those programs where couples on the verge of divorce eventually come to blows. I figured most of the people on those shows must have been actors, even though I knew real couples came to blows too. I'd had an affair with someone. It had ended all at once. In short, sleep had fled from me.

Before packing for our little trip, I called my daughter on the phone. She'd found a job on a farm. Her last postcard had included an inventory of the livestock: "Thirty cows, sixty goats, ten and a half donkeys." The half donkey was a nine-day-old female. Christine hopes to become a veterinarian. At this point in time, she's failed the entrance exam twice. I informed her that I was going to spend a few days at Aunt

Susie's house with Dan. She was quiet for a while. Then, in a playful tone, she said, "I'm sure you two are going to get back together."

She appeared to believe that more than I did. I almost told her I'd changed my mind, I wasn't going to Aunt Susie's, I preferred visiting her, Christine, at her farm. But that wasn't a good idea. Nobody there would have welcomed me with open arms.

"Kiss Daddy for me," Christine said before hanging up.

I packed a bag for three days, threw it on the backseat, and got on the highway, heading north.

Dan arrived after I did. Night had just fallen. You couldn't see the ocean, but you could hear the breaking waves. I was smoking a cigarette in front of the house. When his car turned into the driveway (I recognized the halo around the damaged headlight), I held myself back from rushing over to greet him.

One thing at a time, I thought.

The next day we went walking on the beach. The sky was heavy. A hard wind whipped our clothes and made them billow as though they were inflated.

Dan grimaced.

"What's wrong?"

He'd stopped walking. He bent his left arm and put it behind his back. His fingers struggled to reach his shoulder blade. All that could do was make his pain worse.

"Did you injure yourself?"

"That goddamn . . ."

"Where does it hurt?"

"Everywhere. It hurts there."

His hand fluttered behind his back. I couldn't see the place he was pointing to. I put my hand on his shoulder blade and began to massage him. "You drove all day yesterday," I said. "You must have been hunched over the steering wheel."

"It's not that."

He turned around. I didn't know where to put my hand. It hung in the air before I let it drop.

"It's the mattress," he said.

"The mattress?"

"I couldn't sleep. I tried, but in the end I got up."

I remembered that he'd been sitting in the wicker chair when I woke up.

"You slept in the chair?"

"I didn't sleep. I just sat there."

"Doing what?"

"Nothing. I was watching you."

"You watched me sleep?"

He started walking again. I stayed where I was, imagining the scene. Dan sitting up beside me, like when Christine had a fever. I let him get farther away. Then I followed him, stepping in the footprints he'd just left.

We hadn't spent the previous night in my aunt's house. Uncle Paul slept in the guest room now, while Aunt Susie stayed in their old bedroom. My uncle's sickness didn't allow them to sleep together anymore. Doing so was "risky"— that's the word she'd used. An idiotic vision crossed my mind: Uncle Paul brandishing a knife over the body of his sleeping wife.

Aunt Susie had opened the little house for us, a cottage situated close to the sea. Uncle Paul called it "the cabin." They used to store a small boat and some beach accessories there. The boat was gone, but folding chairs, wooden rackets, and a net rolled into a ball were still piled up in a corner. My aunt's children live far away. They don't come home for holidays. They have small children of their own, and the old folks' house isn't a very attractive destination. In those parts even the summers have something wintry about them.

It was cold in the cabin, especially at night. The evening before, after Dan arrived, I'd loaned him a sweater (I was sure he'd forget to bring one) before lying down on the bed. I was expecting that we'd have a conversation. Not a lengthy thrashing-out, but a brief exchange with the breaking waves in the background. He lay beside me and took my hand. He stroked the finger where I used to wear my wedding band. It wasn't there anymore. I'd taken it off and stuck it in the glove compartment. At the moment, I regretted doing that.

When I opened my eyes again, it was morning. I'd slept with my clothes on. I turned over and saw Dan sitting in the wicker chair. He was smoking (the smell of tobacco had awakened me), and I could barely make out his face. The venetian blinds behind him were parallel, horizontal lines. Dan didn't say a word. I had the impression he didn't see me.

"Did I tell you Christine sends you a kiss?"

"Mm-hmm."

"I spoke to her yesterday."

He exhaled smoke. After a moment he said, "I wrote her before I left. I was answering one of her letters. I wish she wouldn't get her feelings hurt so easily . . ." (He leaned forward. The wicker creaked softly.) " 'Shit, Christine,' I told her, 'when you write a letter, pay attention to your sentences. Use commas, put periods, and I don't know what else. But don't write these twenty-page screeds!' She's twenty years old, for Pete's sake."

"She's not a writer. She's not you."

"It's not a question of writing. It's a question of using short sentences."

Dan stopped talking. I'd turned over on my back. The agreeable sensation that filled me upon waking was gone. I heard the sound of the waves, and I remembered the chaos of our family life. The times when Christine had run away, the way Vincent would look at us when we got drunk in front of him, the parties that never ended and kept him from sleeping. We'd forget to get up and take them to school. One morning, while Dan was speeding along, driving Christine to her singing class, he crashed into a police car. He was sitting in the driver's seat in his underpants. Afterward, he mimicked the expressions on the cops' faces. How we laughed that day. Even Christine, who'd missed her class.

Then everything got worse. It seems crazy that we remained husband and wife. We stayed together for the children, I suppose. Not so we could protect them but so we could protect ourselves. Maintain the illusion that they needed their parents.

My shoes were full of sand. It was more crumbly in Dan's footprints, which were where I was putting my feet. I ended up walking on solid ground.

I didn't want our weekend of patching things up to be ruined. I said, "We can change the mattress."

He looked at me.

"There's another mattress in the garage, leaning against the wall."

A couple of senior citizens passed us on the beach. They had their arms around each other's waists, and the wind was puffing up their clothes just as it was ours. The woman smiled at us. The man flicked his fingers against the visor of his cap. I smiled at them. Dan was looking at the sand.

"Is it an innerspring?"

"What?"

"The mattress in the garage. Is it an innerspring?"

"How should I know?"

"That's what I need. It's not a luxury item," he added, seeing my expression. "Most mattresses are innerspring."

"I find it hard to believe—"

"I'm telling you."

"I find it hard to believe we're talking about mattresses."

I turned around. The senior citizens, no longer strolling along the beach, were walking up to Aunt Susie's house.

"I'm sorry," Dan said.

It seemed to me he wasn't talking about the mattress, he was making a general apology. For having left. For the twenty years that were in the act of slipping through our fingers.

"Chloe—"

"Look."

I'd just noticed the boat that used to be stored in the cabin. It was stranded on the beach a few yards from the waterline.

We exchanged glances. There was a light in Dan's eyes.

I could already see us far from the shore, celebrating our reunion with a little excursion in that boat.

We went over to it and looked inside. The boat's bottom was worm-eaten. Long strips of sand showed through the cracks. In a corner of the boat was a small yellow plastic bucket full of seawater.

"Let's go get the mattress," I said.

We had the whole day in front of us. An entire day to carry the mattress from the garage to the cabin.

The label contained the word "innerspring."

Dan nodded and said, "I told you."

"You think the two of us can carry it?"

"I can carry it by myself."

The mattress looked heavy to me. Especially for someone whose back hurt. When Dan pulled on the side handle, the mattress tipped over onto the garage floor. The top half of the mattress was charred. The fire had apparently been extinguished before it could burn the bottom half.

"Piece of crap," Dan said. "Unusable."

"Why are you saying that? I'm sure we could sleep on it."

"You want to sleep on that thing? Really?"

The fluorescent lights, which we hadn't switched on, began to sizzle. Aunt Susie came into the garage. "Here I am, at your service!" she said.

She strode in with her usual light step, wearing her kitchen apron. My aunt knew that Dan was fond of her shortbread cookies. The visit from her neighbors, the couple we'd seen on the beach, had distracted her from her task.

When we'd arrived back, she'd been just seeing them off. I'd asked her if we could borrow the mattress. All she'd said was, "Go on, I'll be there in a minute."

The fluorescent lights reflected on her brown hair. "I should have warned you," she said. "It's been damaged."

The lilt in her voice contrasted with Dan's sullen demeanor. I elbowed him so he'd make an effort to smile. He gave me an uncomprehending look.

Aunt Susie seemed to want to settle the matter as soon as possible and get back to her cookies.

I said in a jocular tone, "Was someone playing with matches?"

"It was Paul. Ten days ago, he started tinkering with the car engine. He caused a short circuit and something caught fire. The flames blackened the windshield, but fortunately Paul wasn't hurt. I heard him yell and got to him in time. I took down the fire extinguisher and . . ."

We were looking at the mattress.

"It was on the roof of the car," my aunt explained.

The burn mark was shaped like a man's head on an elongated torso.

"It could have been worse."

I was the one who said those words, and I felt stupid.

My aunt winked and said, "Well, we won't be giving him the launch codes."

The wink was addressed to Dan. She was no doubt implying that he should make a story out of the incident. But that wasn't his type of story. He did couples who ruin each other's lives or people who can't manage to stay sober or make a home. He wrote about what he knew. I would have liked it if just for once he would have told a story about Uncle Paul setting off a nuclear war.

I smiled at my aunt to indicate that she was wasting her time, but she'd already turned toward Dan. "Take it if you want it," she said.

After we carried the mattress to the cabin, we went back to the house to eat cookies. It was the first time I'd had a good look at Uncle Paul since the onset of his sickness. The previous evening, I'd seen him through the doorway of his room, sitting on the bed and unbuttoning his shirt. He'd raised his eyes as if he felt himself being watched. I'd waved at him. He hadn't recognized me.

This evening Uncle Paul was in the living room, looking out at the ocean. Toward the horizon the sea was calm, but waves were pounding the shore. At brief intervals, trails of foam ebbed back.

My uncle was a man of imposing size. Aunt Susie used to say he could have been a sports coach. His talent was for training other people. But patience was not his strong point. If you lingered in a restroom, he was the kind of guy who would get tired of waiting for you and drive off. Aunt Susie had once paid the price for staying too long in the ladies' at a highway service area. Now Uncle Paul couldn't go anywhere without her.

When he woke up in the morning, she'd comb his hair. That simple act had become impossible for him. His face had the expression of someone waiting for the punch line of a joke. He'd look at you with his mouth slightly open. You'd feel obliged to put on the same look. Or to tell a story and defer its ending so he'd have reasons to be continually surprised.

He was still able to talk. He'd speak his questions out loud. He'd wonder where he'd parked the car (he never mentioned the garage) or whether someone would come and get him at a given time (my aunt was the only person taking care of him) or who was going to come and when.

Very quickly, we all had cookies in our mouths. Dan swallowed two at once.

I turned to my uncle and said, "We found the boat this morning."

He screwed up his eyes.

"It had a little bucket in it. A yellow bucket."

Dan asked my aunt, "Did it belong to your children?"

I wanted Dan to address at least a few words to my uncle, the beginnings of a conversation, but Dan didn't understand. I frowned. He took a paper napkin from the coffee table. His knees were covered with cookie crumbs.

Aunt Susie got up to serve the tea.

"A yellow bucket? Someone must have forgotten it. Who takes milk?"

I waved the milk off. Dan held out his cup. My aunt looked at him benevolently. "What are you writing at the moment?"

"At the moment, I'm not writing anything."

"He's going to a colloquium."

My voice had turned shrill, as if I was announcing an exploit.

"A meeting of writers?"

"No," Dan said, sounding apologetic. "University professors. They study my short stories and see things in them I didn't see when I wrote them."

"Impressive."

I glanced at my uncle. For an instant, I thought he looked the way he'd looked in former days. He was keeping his mouth closed. He seemed attentive.

Dan put his hands on his knees. Then he spoke, a little more softly than before: "When I went to AA meetings, everyone told their story. The rest of us listened. We recognized ourselves in the other people's stories."

My aunt and I exchanged glances. Dan had taken me by surprise. I'd never mentioned his drinking problem to Aunt Susie. I'd been silent about my own troubles with alcohol, too. Drinking with your husband in order to feel less alone had turned out to be a bad move.

Then something happened. Uncle Paul sat forward on his chair. He planted his feet solidly and waggled his fingers. His tongue lolled out as he tapped hard on the empty air. Every time his index fingers struck the invisible keys, he made a moist, salivating sound. Each sound corresponded to a keystroke. Not only was this a funny sight, but his movements were also somehow graceful.

He was imitating Dan at his typewriter: not just a drunken man but a man determined to stay the course despite the state into which drink had plunged him.

Uncle Paul knew more about Dan than I thought.

We sat staring, our cups suspended in midair, utterly surprised to see my uncle revive before our eyes.

During those few seconds, it seemed to me that nothing was tragic, that with a little goodwill we could overcome everything. I took Dan's hand and squeezed it.

Dan stroked my hand as he'd done the night before, his fingers passing over mine, feeling for the wedding ring.

It was still in the glove compartment, but a vision from I don't know where rose before my eyes, and I saw my wedding ring floating in the yellow bucket and the bottom of the boat covered with sand and water, which ebbed and flowed and made the wedding ring, the bucket, the whole boat shake.

"Dinner was delicious. Like the whole day. What a delicious day. Your aunt is a delicious person."

"You're talking like Gertrude Stein."

Having said yes to everything my aunt had proposed to pour for me, I'd returned to the cabin fairly tipsy. Dan had drunk nothing but water.

My remark made him smile. When we were students, one of our games consisted of repeating the same word from one sentence to the next, as Gertrude Stein did in her stories.

Dan's smile vanished. "I'm tired," he said. "I feel better than I did this morning, but I'm tired. This morning I had a backache, but I wasn't tired."

He fell silent. I was sitting on the edge of the bed, unbuttoning my sweater. Dan lay on the burned mattress.

In a hesitant voice, he said, "I hope we can love each other."

The only light in the cabin came from a little lamp at the foot of the bed. I couldn't make out Dan's features.

Was he talking about loving each other though separated or loving each other and staying together?

"Do you want to sleep with me?"

He was out of the bed now, standing beside the innerspring mattress and waiting for my answer.

I pricked up my ears for the sound of the sea.

You would have thought it had receded altogether.

I slept beside Dan on the innerspring. Or rather I snuggled up against him and waited for sleep to come.

The sound of the breaking waves returned with obsessive regularity. I set myself to counting them.

I felt Dan's breath on my neck. Like a current of warm air filtering under the door. I forbade myself to stir, to make the slightest movement. I didn't want to awaken him.

The minutes, the hours went by.

I counted to a hundred and then back to one without putting myself to sleep. Sentences began to form in my head. Then they crumbled away like sand castles.

At the end of what seemed like an eternity, I turned over abruptly, determined to wake Dan up so he'd stop breathing down my neck.

But he wasn't snuggled against me. He was sitting in the wicker chair.

I pushed away the hair blocking my sight. When my eyes grew accustomed to the darkness, I saw that Dan was staring into space, as frightened as if he'd just learned that his days were numbered.

I stretched out my arms to him.

"I'm here," I said. "Don't you see me? I'm here. My love. I'm here."

JOANNE

On Saturday we take up our posts at O'Brien's, an Irish pub a few steps from our house. We sit in a corner and set to work. Each of us has a copy of the story. I drink tea. Raymond has apple juice, which is the color of whiskey.

"'The Mattress.' You're sure about the title?"

"Positive."

"But is the mattress at the heart of the story? Besides, what kind of mattress are we talking about?"

At first he thinks I'm joking. Then he realizes I'm not going to let anything pass.

"They talk about an innerspring."

"Then you should call it 'Innerspring.'" I scratch out the original title.

"'The Innerspring,' then," Raymond says.

"I think 'Innerspring' is very good."

He laughs his little laugh.

"What's funny?"

His face melts me, but I'm not about to relent. I say, "Are we playing or are we working?"

"I'm sorry, it's just that . . . it's the title Douglas would have chosen."

He stops laughing and concentrates on the story. I emulate him. The manuscript of Raymond's collection, sent back by Douglas, is under my copy of "Innerspring." Douglas's manuscript bears no trace of his cuts. The edited text is clean, unmarked, retyped at Raymond's expense. I've checked the number of pages. More than half have disappeared.

I didn't dare tell him. I was evasive. "His cuts aren't all bad," I said, trying to spare him a shock. If he saw them, he'd start drinking again.

At the end of several minutes, he looks up at me and says, "Have you finished going through Douglas's manuscript?"

"Raymond. We're correcting 'Innerspring.'"

"Sorry, I lost focus." He turns his attention back to the story. "'Innerspring,'" he says, his voice trailing off. "Why not?" He sips his apple juice and makes a note of the new title.

When he puts down his glass, he notices the envelope. "Say, what's in there?"

"Hands off!" I say, tapping his fingers.

"Joanne—"

"I'll show it to you later."

"How many cuts?"

"Later, I said."

He wants to know. The most I can do is delay the moment a little.

"Raymond, you say it yourself: You have to revise a story while it's still warm."

I don't like the expression on his face. His left eyebrow's more furrowed than usual. Like he was ogling a bottle of gin.

I'm afraid he's going to snatch the envelope away from me, but I don't put my hand on it. Let him decide.

He smiles and looks toward the bar.

I should be relieved, but I remain tense. My eyes go back to "Innerspring." The page with the last words is sticking out from under the rest of the pages.

"Let's start at the end," I say.

"The end?"

"The final sentences."

He picks up the page and begins to read slowly. "'I'm here . . . Don't you see me? I'm here. My l—'"

"'My love. I'm here,'" I say, finishing it for him so it won't take two hours.

"You don't like the ending?"

"I think we can get rid of the third 'I'm here,' don't you?"

"Wait," he says, looking at the page.

I start to lose patience. "The reader understands she's there. No need to say it three times!"

I pick up my pencil and strike the third "I'm here." I press so hard the lead breaks, leaving a zigzag mark on the page.

I look at Raymond out of the corner of my eye. He's gazing at the envelope.

I say, "And you know what? I almost feel like striking 'My love,' too."

"Striking it?"

"I don't see what it's doing there."

"It's what she feels."

I'm waiting for his tongue to slip, I'm waiting for him to tell me, "It's what Marianne feels."

"As far as I'm concerned, she's not in love anymore. Yes, she wants to save her marriage. She's hanging on to that. But there can't be any more talk of love. If the story ends with that word—"

"It ends with 'I'm here.'"

"She's there, but her love for him, that's gone. It's run away, it's flown off!" I say, flinging my hands in the air. "That's what the story's about, isn't it?"

He rubs the back of his neck. "It's more complicated than that," he says. "As far as I'm concerned, there's some ambiguity."

"That's the whole question."

He looks up at me. I raise my teacup and hide behind it.

Raymond turns a few pages. "Show me the places where the ambiguity poses a problem."

I sit back in my chair and start to go over the story again. But I can't concentrate. Or rather, I focus on details. I search for proof that this story is truer than the others.

Is he still in love with her?

I look at him.

He's not paging through the story anymore. He's filched the envelope Douglas sent.

"Raymond!"

He winks at me, holds up the envelope, and slips out the manuscript.

I heave a sigh. I'm afraid for him, for us.

He mutters, "I can't let him do this," and turns over the cover page.

RAYMOND

"July 8, 7 a.m."

Should I put the time or not? What'll he think if I do? He'll think I'm a wreck. Ah well, let him think that, since it's the case.

"Dearest Douglas, You have to get me out of . . . I have to get out of this. I'm going to explain and you'll understand. Things have never seemed so clear to me."

May as well lay it all out.

"Even though I didn't sleep last night. I've been rereading the manuscript and looking at your changes, your amputations, your . . ."

He calls them cuts. Better just write "your cuts" so as not to antagonize him.

"I've read over all the stories and examined every sentence, I've consulted the original texts and compared the two versions, yours and mine."

Watch out here. Kid gloves.

"Yours is often better than mine."

Tell him that so he'll listen to the rest.

"Douglas, listen to me, I've reread the manuscript until the letters jumped off the page and started vibrating in front of my face. Not an hour ago, I was still shooing them away like flies. If Joanne had woken up, she would have called the emergency number and I would have wound up in the same medical center as I did

two years ago. The one that used to be a hospital for the criminally insane. You could see their names carved into the linoleum with knives, and their obscene drawings . . ."

What's got into me, telling him that? Besides, it's not true. The medical center was built only recently. I'm writing a short story.

"*But now I can see clearly. I don't want my stories to be published in their present form. (Did you edit 'Mine'? It looks as though you didn't—I counted the same number of words as in my version.) Put simply, they're no longer my stories. I recognize something very dark in them that resembles my past life, but I don't see myself in them as I am today. I've come through all that. I sure came close to not making it, but if there's one thing this collection—in my version—shows, it's that I've come through. I didn't write twenty-two short stories as hard-edged as despair. I don't know where that despair comes from, Douglas. Is it yours?*"

Christ. I tell him that and I'm dead. He'll scrap my stories. I have to win him over, soften him up with compliments.

"*Cutting the last five pages of 'Think Twice' (which you've renamed 'Fill It with Super') so that it ends just when the guy finds himself alone in the middle of the desert—you ought to get a medal for that, the Astutest Editor Award. But that's just it, it's not mine. It's too brilliant to be mine.*"

Precisely, he'll reply. Precisely.

"*I know you're going to think I'm an ingrate. I'm not forgetting that you've spent long hours, maybe even entire nights, revising these stories to make them better. They've cost you time and money. I want you to know that I've just placed the check, the generous advance you procured for me, in an envelope, and I'm prepared to return it to you.*"

That makes me think . . . The check I mailed him to cover his typing expenses is sure to bounce. Let's wait until he asks me for the money. Don't make a move until he asks for it.

"Now I fear the worst. If just one of my stories were to be published in your version, I think I'd be blocked again, incapable of writing. Yes, that's what I'm afraid of."

And look at this, I'm starting to shake.

"You have to understand: I've escaped from the grave. I had one foot in it already, thanks to alcohol, but these stories saved me, they got me out. They're the proof that I survived. DO YOU UNDERSTAND?"

No, no all caps. Strike that. Makes me sound like my back's against the wall.

"That's why I'm dedicating the collection to Joanne."

Why bring that up? He'll take it badly. He loves when the books he's butchered are dedicated to him.

"Douglas, if you could publish my stories as I wrote them, correct them a little, improve them without changing them entirely, if you could be content with doing that, I wouldn't have this feeling that I'm in danger . . ."

Good grief, I'm getting paranoid. A case of acute paranoia.

"God Almighty, Douglas, please get me out of this.

"Raymond

"P.S. You understand me, don't you? I'm asking you to stop production on my short-story collection. I hope you'll forgive me."

Not humble enough. Too short and not sufficiently humble. I'll toss it and start over. I can write it straight out and have it finished before the mailman comes. Already eight o'clock. Twenty cigarettes in one hour. Joanne's still asleep.

I've got to finish this letter and mail it before she wakes up and sees me in this state.

"July 8, 8 a.m. Dearest Douglas . . ."

DOUGLAS

His July 8 letter. The long supplication of Raymond. I read it, of course. I read it, but I didn't heed it.

Heeding it would have been a mistake.

Don't get too close to your authors; if you do, they'll make you pay.

They'll drag you into considerations that aren't and shouldn't be yours.

Ray can't unilaterally interrupt a process I've put my whole weight, my whole reputation into.

My blood, my sweat.

His collection has to appear with all my revisions, just as they are. It has to appear minus the passages I've cut, whether he wants it to or not. As for his letter . . .

I was about to tear it up, but I've changed my mind.

It would have been a mistake.

There's a market for authors' letters. Even when they're badly written.

*

Ray's story collection was published on July 20, as scheduled.

Never, not even in my wildest dreams, would I have imagined a success of this magnitude.

Raymond's been launched. He's in orbit. He won't be coming back down.

Sometimes I find my power frightening.

Yes, sometimes I can't fathom it myself.

RAYMOND

The only one of my stories he didn't touch is called "Mine." It's the tale of a couple who are fighting over a baby. In the end, they start pulling on it. They nearly cut it in half.

That story he didn't touch. At least I don't think he did.

DOUGLAS

I touched "Mine." The last sentence went, "This was how they resolved the question." *They resolved the question . . .* that declaration bothered me for an entire day.

"This was how the question was resolved."

After I wrote that, I felt better.

RAYMOND

The first article said, "He pares and shaves his prose like a whittler with a knife." The following articles took up that remark. They all passed it back and forth.

As if there was nothing more fabulous than whittling.

The misunderstanding has taken hold without my being able to do a thing about it.

DOUGLAS AND RAYMOND

It's the beginning of winter. The city looks like a black-and-white photograph. Everything seems rigid, paralyzed by fog. *Postmen like doctors go from house to house.* And I'm weighed down with manuscripts.

Winter makes me melancholy. I don't read as fast as I do in autumn, and my approach is generally more indulgent. If your work tends toward pathos, write me in the winter. You'll have more of a chance. I'll let your metaphors live. You'll have the right to use an adverb. You can even employ the word "soul." But don't get carried away. In the spring I return to zero tolerance.

Past four o'clock. Raymond should be here any minute.

Ever since he stopped drinking, he prides himself on being punctual. It's no longer necessary to organize a search for him because he's dead drunk in some bar. "Alive, sober, and working." That's how he described himself in a letter to me. "Loving and loved by a good woman." His Anne Sexton wannabe. "Why shouldn't I have a right to happiness?" It's the new Raymond. A guy who has rights.

Clearly, the time has come to renegotiate.

His contract is going to expire. While rights to his short stories are being sold to half the globe, I've had the agreement that binds us rewritten. And I've doubled his advance. I'm no fool, I'm not going to saw off the branch I'm . . .

In short, I intend to keep him.

"Raymond."

"Douglas."

"You're wearing a tie? I barely recognized you."

"It's Joanne. She insisted I wear her father's tie."

"You don't see that kind very often."

"People turn around in the street."

"You can take it off. We just won't say anything to Joanne."

He keeps his tie on, as if I've been talking to the wall.

"Nice office."

"This is the first time you've been here?"

"Mm-hmm."

"Just think, we've done everything by mail."

"*You've* done everything," he mutters. He sits down and points a finger at the computer. "Hell of a machine."

"Not my thing. I do all my corrections by hand."

"Well, one doesn't change—"

"A winning team."

That wasn't what he was going to say. He was going to say "old habits."

We stare at each other. I turn to the computer and say, "My secretary showed me one of its functions."

He seems as enthralled as if I were talking to him about my psoriasis.

"I can do this on any text." I show him what I mean. "You see?"

"It's crossed out."

"Yeah. I crossed out the word. And if I want, I can do this."

"Incredible."

"Crossed out twice."

"I can see it."

"'Double strikethrough,' it's called."

"And the first one?"

"'Single strikethrough.'"

"Obviously."

"But I don't give a shit about that. I do everything by hand."

"Hell of a machine," he says again.

That's what I like about Raymond. He cuts to the chase. Not one word too many. Except in his short stories.

"Serious matters," I say.

"Now?"

"Now."

"I saw André in the lobby."

I let my surprise show. "That little jerk?"

"I like him."

"You don't know André. He's a hungry young editor on the make. But at the first obstacle, he's going to be sobbing into his secretary's skirt. They don't give him anything but second novels."

"Oh, no?"

"There's nothing to be done for second novels. Nobody reads them. They get passed to profit and loss."

"They get passed to André—"

"They get passed to André, who puts them in the loss column."

"I didn't know that."

"Third novels wind up on my desk. Look." (I point to a manuscript as thick as a telephone book.) "It's Eleanor's."

"I'm eager to read it."

"It's the story of a nun during the Second World War. She paints watercolors while the world goes up in smoke."

"You think it'll do well?"

I sigh and say, "Things have changed quite a bit since your last visit."

"You don't have your rose window anymore."

"I sold it."

"Get a good price?"

"You may not believe me, but it wasn't worth a dime."

"You should have told me about it. There's a church near us that would have bought that window from you."

"Really?"

"Joanne and I would have bought it from you. The window in my office faces south. I would have taken that window off your hands."

"It's true that you're rich now."

"I wouldn't say that."

"Well, you're on the way to being rich."

"My family . . . my ex-family is bleeding me dry."

"Not for long."

I hand him eight sheets of paper stapled together.

"What's this?"

"The contract for your next collection."

He huddles back in his chair.

"Where's my pen? I have a hundred manuscripts and no pen."

I rummage around in my coat pockets and take out the felt-tip pen I use to make my cuts. He recognizes it.

"The murder weapon," I say.

He doesn't laugh. He says, "I've signed on with André."

"You just sign your name. I'll initial it for you."

He looks at me. After a delay, I register what he's just said.

"André's my new editor."

I put the felt-tip away. I loosen my shirt collar and scratch the irritated skin on the back of my neck. Then I go and sit down at my desk.

"You know what the people here say about me?"

The light streaming in from outside dazzles him. He blinks.

"They say I'm paranoid."

"Douglas—"

"Yeah. Paranoid. Now let me ask you a question. Am I looking at a friend?"

He says nothing. He's waiting for me to go on.

"Or an enemy?"

More blinking.

"Betrayal, Raymond. There's nothing I detest more than betrayal."

"I haven't betrayed you. I've been intending to change ever since—"

"You're changing sides at the moment of victory."

He says nothing.

"You see this contract? Watch what I do with it."

I take a pair of scissors and cut the contract into strips. I gather a handful of strips and cut them up some more.

He stands. "There's no need for you to do that," he says.

I put down my scissors. "It's a gesture of trust, Ray. The bond between you and me is stronger than any contract. Why did you sign with André?"

"I don't want you cutting me anymore."

"Listen to me. I can see you're in one of your moods. Honestly, you ought to sit back down, take a tranquilizer, and think things over."

"I don't want you cutting me anymore."

I let a few seconds go by.

"Do you know they want to fire me?"

"That's a joke, right?"

"No, they're trying to get rid of me. My position is hanging by a thread. If your story collection hadn't been a success, they would have shown me the door long before this."

"Well, fortunately they didn't."

"Bullshit! You waited until my back was turned and then signed with the competition!"

"I'm not changing houses. Just editors."

"You waited until I was dead!"

"I told André I could stay with you."

"Really?"

"Provided you limit yourself to copyediting."

"What did he say?"

"He said you'd refuse."

"He got that right. You think I'm going to work for that fool? Be his assistant?"

"Of course not."

Raymond heads for the door.

The walls seem to be approaching each other. It looks like they're closing in on me.

"I know what I owe you, Douglas."

I spin around toward the window. "You don't owe me anything. Except minimalism."

"What does that mean?"

"I've whispered that word to the press. Invented a school."

"I'm anything but a minimalist."

I turn my face to him. "Even in betrayal? What school do you belong to in the art of betrayal?"

"Go fuck yourself, Douglas."

He leaves.

That can't have happened. I can't have lost Raymond. I stand up, I totter among my manuscripts.

I reach a spot in the middle of the office, stiffen myself, mop my forehead.

And I smile. Yes, there's a smile on my face. I glimpse Raymond's future. His manuscripts published uncut, just as they are. That's what's waiting for him if he dumps me.

I charge into the hall and yell at him, "YOU'RE FUCKED, RAY, YOU HEAR ME? STARTING TODAY, YOU'RE DEAD!"

I run out of breath and continue in a lower voice, alone in the hall: "*Finis.*"

All at once it dawns on me that he never uses Latin in his short stories. Not even the easiest word to understand: *Finis.*

Almost five o'clock. If I left now, I wouldn't come across a single mailman. But they must be somewhere. With their mailbags full of manuscripts. Bundles of short stories, the hope of someone's life.

How can anyone place so much hope in short stories? How is that possible?

I should never have sold my rose window.

MARIANNE

How could a person die so senselessly?

Nobody deserves an end like that.

What saddens me the most is that he never wrote me. I could have told him . . . I could have warned him against those people.

No, I don't think it was his decision. I think he was manipulated. He met up with a guru. Some guy stronger than he was. Even so, seventy people, and they all died in the fire. No. I don't think they've identified his body. One of the investigators told me, "The problem with sects is they burn their records. The archives go up in flames along with the members." That contributes to their mystique, he explained.

Crazy, huh?

I knew Edgar was a mystic, but I didn't think he was nuts.

So what are you doing for her birthday? She's three, I can't get over it. Oh, don't say "young," don't say I'm a "young grandmother." I feel old. Even more so since . . . You talked to him? How's he doing? No, I haven't heard from him since . . . He's been out of the country. He always is, I believe.

With that tramp.

Do you know I spoke to her two months ago? My bad luck. I called up to talk to Raymond and she answered the phone. Yes, I know they're living together, but all the same. I have every right not to get used to it.

Anyway, I call up and that tramp answers. I try to be polite and not gnash my teeth. But after a few minutes I can't hold out any longer, and I say, "I'm surprised Ray doesn't want to see his family more often." I emphasize *more often*, like I'm wondering what in the world the reason could be. And you know what she says? No joking, you know what she says? She says, "Ray has to leave the elements of his past life behind. That's the condition for him to stay sober." She dared to tell me that! "Look," I say, "are you calling me an element? My name's Marianne. It isn't gin or Scotch or vodka."

And then I hung up on her, but she hung up before I did.

I love this place. Everything's so calm here. Have I told you how much the chestnut tree has grown? You have to come here with the little one. I'm going to have a swing installed in the backyard. You could all come. Leo and Greta, you and Chris, all my grandchildren. Three generations around the chestnut tree. We could invite Raymond. After he gets back.

I know. She'd never let him come.

I feel a little lonely, to tell you the truth. In spite of the people who stay here. "Spiritual coach," that's how I present myself. I listen to their problems, I identify whatever's not going right. Sometimes they ask me, "How about you? How did you manage to pull through?"

I'm not so sure I've pulled through.

I read Ray's stories and I realize he's never stopped writing about us, about him and me. He reopens our wounds. He displays them to the whole world, and the whole world applauds.

That's what's called fiction, but readers forget there are people behind it. Readers forget the elements of the fiction.

No, I haven't pulled through.

It's my success, too. It's ours, you know. Your father's success is ours.

Even if we'll never see any money.

JOANNE

April 30

I'm writing this in the garden of the Hotel de Russie, a haven of peace in the heart of Rome. Ray hasn't gotten up yet. Last night's dinner exhausted him.

Magdalena, his Italian translator, served as our interpreter. When the three editors seated near us started to quarrel over the rights to Ray's next story collection, we retreated to a corner to talk with her. To our amazement, this petite and very lively lady turned out to have been Hemingway's translator too. She described in great detail her meeting with him sometime in the 1950s. As we listened to her, I felt as though we were on a boat headed out to sea. With Hemingway at the helm.

Ray devoured the puntarelle *and asked for a second helping of the truffle risotto. I pointed out to him that we weren't at an all-you-can-eat buffet, but Magda encouraged us to make ourselves at home. I told her we didn't eat that well at home. Ray's appetite always surprises me. He needs to compensate for the lack of sugar.*

He smokes too much. I tell him it's not real smart to stop destroying yourself with your right hand if you're just going to speed up the process with your left. He's right-handed, but he uses his left hand when he smokes. I'd like to write a poem on that subject—I'll call it "Smoking Left-handed."

Yesterday he explained to a journalist that alcoholism was doubtless a metaphor for his social condition. The journalist pretended he understood what Ray was talking about, but Ray looked at me as if he himself didn't. He loathes interviews. He feels obliged to come up with statements people will want to quote, whereas in his stories he avoids that sort of thing like the plague.

The day we arrived, while he was taking a nap, I went out and explored the neighborhood. I discovered a little bookstore behind the Trevi Fountain (I'll go back there tomorrow and get the name of the street). A very old man wearing spectacles was the shopkeeper. I could hardly make out his eyes through the lenses, which were as thick as magnifying glasses. On a table where books were spread out in a disorderly jumble, I found a volume of Cesare Pavese's poems. I copied out a few lines in my notebook:

> Verrà la morte e avrà i tuoi occhi—
> questa morte che ci accompagna
> dal mattino alla sera, insonne . . .

I told myself I'd give the volume to Raymond as a present, even though he doesn't understand a word of Italian. Poetry's never as beautiful as it is in the languages one doesn't know. When I realized I didn't have enough money on me, I put the book back where I'd found it. I wasn't actually unhappy to leave it behind, because the poem in question talks about . . .

And I've always been superstitious.

RAYMOND

I'd never have thought it could be so short. It's true I had a premonition. I even wanted to get it over with, more than once. But I'd put that off until tomorrow. Like with drinking. For ten or fifteen years, I'd think, *That's enough. I'm stopping.* I'd admonish myself: *You hear, Ray? This is the last of a long line. After this one, you're stopping.* I'd pour another drink and make a silent declaration: *Tomorrow, I'm stopping.* I persuaded myself that each drink was the last. But there was always a tomorrow, and life would start over again.

I've just been told it won't be starting over anymore.

Sometimes, when fear loosens its grip, curious thoughts arise in me. Like bubbles.

This one, for example: *Good thing I write short stories.* If they were novels, I'd feel I was being interrupted in the middle. There's a novel I've always wanted to write, but alcohol stood in the way. Short pieces were all I could manage.

Yet I don't want to give up on that novel. I feel like starting work on it even if I have to die tomorrow. It would be a way of protesting, a refusal to be a pushover.

Tackling a novel when you're at the end of the road, writing the first sentence on the day you're condemned to death—what could be more human than that?

And the bubbles expand; they become hope.

MARIANNE AND RAYMOND

"Are you in pain?" I ask him on the telephone.

"They say I'll be in even more pain if they interrupt the treatment. But what's the use of continuing the treatment if . . . What's the use?"

"There must still be some hope. Don't you want me to come?"

"What's the use?"

I say it again: "Don't you want me to come?"

"What's the use?" he repeats.

The same words with a different meaning.

He lets a few seconds pass. Then he says, "Disease is making me a minimalist."

"No it isn't. You're anything but a minimalist."

That makes him laugh. I regret the remark instantly, because it hurts him to laugh.

We keep talking. I do my best not to make him laugh again, but once or twice I can't stop myself.

He didn't marry me for nothing.

RAYMOND

When my daughter was born, my father was a patient in the same hospital. One floor up. He was gravely ill. The day Marianne had the baby, he came close to breathing his last. A birth, a death. Tit for tat. He passed away a few years later.

If Leo's wife were about to have a baby one floor down, I'd prefer not to know it. I'd be glad to hear it, but I'd just as soon not be told. Or be told later.

The truth is, at the baby's first cry I'd have the feeling I should hurry up and complete the exchange. I'd hear the creditor knocking on my door.

Ah, I sound like I'm dead already. But in fact I'm still alive. As long as it doesn't get into my brain, I'll stay alive. That's what they told me this morning. "Above all, we want to prevent it from going to your head."

I told them not to worry. I've always been humble, I said. It's true, ask your friends. They'll say, "Whatever happens to him, nothing goes to his head."

I've got my first sentence.

If there was one thing people appreciated about him, it was that nothing went to his head.

No.

If there's one thing . . . appreciate about him . . . nothing goes to his head.

It's better in the present. If Douglas were here, he'd put it in the present.

"I always tell my students, and I'm telling you, Ray: Never forget the virtues of the present."

Frigging Douglas.

I would never have thought it could be so short and so good all the same.

But there are a great many things one has no idea of.

JOANNE

The big day sure is sad.

I insisted on making this trip. I thought it would do him good. Which seems to be the case, but I didn't think I'd be so sad.

Raymond's looking mischievous. A rascal wearing a cap and gown who slips in among the professors. He's going to be made a doctor *honoris causa*. He'll be going home with a diploma, a fine parchment inscribed in Latin.

The trees on this campus are magnificent. How can the school afford to maintain them? Stupid question. One student's tuition would pay three gardeners' salaries.

I would have liked to be a student here. To walk across

these quads with my arms full of books, under the eyes of these marble statues. That looks like a stucco column, that last one. All these statues. Not many of women. Show me one that's not Venus or Galatea, just one woman men's eyes haven't petrified into myth, and I could walk through their little courtyards whistling. It seems they have one of Anne Sexton's manuscripts. I'll go and see it after the reception.

In the airplane he said, "You'll have to address me as 'Doctor' now." I burst out laughing. He grimaced slightly and added, "Just when I learn I'm incurable, they give me a doctorate. Life has a hell of a sense of humor, don't you think?"

We were about to land. I looked at the houses on the hillside. All of them built on the same model.

I turned to him. He went on: "It's curious, the way life makes fun of us. But you know what? I don't hold that against it." He looked out the airplane window. "No, I don't hold even that against it."

It's almost his turn. I should have brought a better camera. These throwaway things, you never know what they're going to give you. They say "throwaway" without explaining that what you'll throw away will be the photographs. There's Ray, here he comes.

My God, how thin he is.

RAYMOND

I'm writing a story that takes place after my death.

The setting is a wake. Some people get together after the death of a friend and recollect a bunch of things about him. At the beginning, good feelings predominate. But it all degenerates pretty quickly.

The dead guy could be me. He's not me, of course, but he could be.

I'm taking a strange pleasure in writing this story. Having started it, I find I can't stop. Maybe it will become a novel. I've written seventy-two short stories. Seventy-two little inspirations before getting my breath. Who can top that?

As for this story, I don't want anybody cutting it. I won't let anyone touch it. I just finished a story about Chekhov's last hours. Joanne's looking it over. But this story, the one that begins after my death, I'm not going to show her. It would make her too sad.

No revising, no corrections. I just hope I can finish it. In some way it's a wager.

As long as I write, I stay alive.

JOANNE

He writes all day and doesn't sleep at night. At night, his illness wakes up. He gets out of bed, gropes his way through the darkness, and shuts himself up in the bathroom. I hear him coughing in there.

He coughs hard enough to rip his lungs apart.

He says the coughing is a protest against the disease. If he stops coughing, he's afraid his brain will take it as a signal. As if the cough said to the brain, "The body's putting up a fight. You have to fight too." So he puts all his energy into coughing.

My God, why does he have to go? He's only just found his way, he's found it at my side.

He says, "Complaining doesn't do any good. You just have to be ready." I pretend to be. To accompany him, I pretend to be as ready as he is.

Before going to sleep we watched *King Solomon's Mines*. I'd never seen it before. The movie opens with the death of an elephant. I don't know if they actually killed one or not, but the scene is grippingly real. There are sunsets and a bush fire that puts the animals to flight in a deafening stampede across the savanna. Ray was like a child, watching that.

Afterward he slept a little. I heard him talking in his sleep. He kept repeating Marianne's name.

At eight o'clock I bring him his coffee. I say, "You talked in your sleep last night. I heard part of your dream."

"Really?"

He examines the inside of his coffee cup.

"Maybe you remember some bits of it?"

I don't mention Marianne. He swallows a mouthful and looks at his cup. Like he was going to find his dream there. "No," he says. "I don't remember anything."

I go down to the living room and take up the poem I started last evening. No words come to me. I lay the poem aside and go back upstairs to the study.

Ray's sitting there surrounded by his library. He's correcting a manuscript. I don't know which one.

It occurs to me that his little secrets are multiplying. "All right," I say, beside myself. "This dream. What was it?"

He looks at me. Immediately I regret what I said. I start

searching for the words to apologize with. At that moment, he says, "Fine. I'm going to tell you my dream." He taps the pages he's correcting. "As soon as I finish revising, I'll tell you."

I nod my head as if he has no choice and turn on my heels.

On the stairs I hear him coughing.

When I go into the kitchen, I can't hear him anymore.

I have doubts. I feel I've been horrible. I have no right to invite myself into his dreams. I bite my lips and dash back upstairs to apologize as abjectly as I can.

My footsteps pound the floor like the buffalo hooves in last night's film.

When I stick my head through the little window at the top of the stairs, I don't see him. His chair is empty.

I detect his respiration, his labored breathing.

I turn my head and call, "Ray!"

I'm not ready, you know.

DOUGLAS

Thank you. Thank you, everyone.

Colleagues, friends, enemies, there are a great many of you here, and I like to think, yes, I like to think you've come on my account.

I'm the star attraction this evening, am I not?

I've been given this trophy—it's in the form of a spear or maybe a feather duster—in any case this thing has been bestowed on me as an award for my whole career, as if it were over. That goes straight to my heart. This spear of yours goes straight to my heart, no joke. Oops, I'm not doing a very good job of remaining upright.

I'm very sorry to disappoint you, but my career isn't finished. I bend but I don't break. A number of times, I've been pushed out . . . and every time I've bounced back. I've taken my authors with me. I'd like to hear even one of you say you regret coming along.

I'm waiting to see some hands. Richard? Of course not, Richard, you've got every reason to thank me. Nicole? We could have done great things together, Nicole, but you went and did some very small ones with the competition. Pardon my vodka, I mean, my frankness.

And since this is a time for sincerity, since I no longer feel bound by any ties to the enterprise for which I nearly ruined the best years of my youth, to "the sprawling organization that provided me with the pittance on which I survived," since the house is on fire and the books are going up in smoke—you will note that the editor may be sacked and removed from the fire, but who will stop the books from burning? Eh, Paul? I love your tie.

I'm fascinated by the neckties writers wear to big occasions. The perfection of a writer's knot betrays the fact that someone else has tied it for him.

Where was I? Ah yes, frankness.

Frankness requires that I reveal the circumstances in which a writer like Raymond—are you here, Ray? Are you part of this sparkling, tie-wearing, comic gathering? If you are, I'd appreciate it if you'd tell the assembly how I rewrote your short stories. With what consummate art . . .

Tell them, tell them you're my creation.

At the moment when the house is burning, when books are getting as stale as old soda water, reveal to us how a work of fiction is built.

The only trophy I'm interested in accepting is the trophy for being the greatest literary ventriloquist of my generation.

Your trophy, this double-feathered spear, I leave to you.

I already have enough things to polish at home.

*

So how was I? Did I talk loud enough? Good. At one point, I was afraid they were going to cut the mike.

More vodka, please. No. Wait. My flask. Take it out of my pocket. Not that one, that's oil for scales. *Scales.* Shit. Nobody here speaks my language. Nobody's equipped to understand me.

That's a cute skirt you're wearing. Do you say *slit skirt*? What's the word? The exact word? I'd say *uncinched*.

Huh? What's that you're saying? Ray? He's . . . You're talking about Raymond? You're fucking kidding me. It's Raymond you're talking about?

Shit.

JOANNE |

A year has passed. And I still haven't started to live again.

What sustains me is my mission. To make his work known. I can't imagine a lovelier task. Do I say that because

I have no choice? It fell to me. Sometimes the best thing that can happen is to have no choice.

Every day I find stories among his papers. As if he were still here, still writing. And of course, that means I have decisions to make. To make alone. This story, for example. It could be the first chapter of a novel. Unless I take out the last few pages and stop the story at the moment when Iris rejoins the others inside the house.

If I cut it off at that point, it becomes a short story. Its title could be "The Drink That Did Him In."

What do you think about that, Ray?

The idea that Douglas is going to enter this house fills me with a strange excitement.

I feel like the torero we saw in Mexico. When the moment for the deathblow came, Ray didn't want to look. "You have too much heart," I said, teasing him. The crowd roared. He kept his hand over his eyes.

Me, I kept mine wide open.

JOANNE AND DOUGLAS

When I open the door, a draft of air comes in with him. The wind chimes, five silver tubes, panic more severely than usual.

Douglas looks over at them.

"They come from Uzbekistan," I tell him.

"You can also find them not far from my apartment."

It's Douglas, no doubt. His thin lips strike a line through the lower part of his face. His eyes transfix from a distance.

His long silvery locks fall to his shoulders and give him a semblance of style. But Douglas isn't a dandy. The purpose of his linen clothes is not to soften the contact between the world and him, it's to make the contact between his clothes and his skin bearable. The perimeter of his affection spreads no farther than that.

I show him to a seat in the living room. When I come back from the kitchen with tea and cakes, he's contemplating the oblique panel that opens to the sky. It's as though he wants to drink the light. His movements are slow and stiff. I feel like I'm receiving a Sioux chieftain. I notice his wide belt, as tanned as his skin. When you get close to him, you breathe in a smell of leather mixed with an aggressive, repellent scent. A bouquet of glass and metal.

"What are these?"

"Lemon and poppy seed."

He inhales and takes a cake. "Ray told me you were an excellent cook."

He doesn't remember having dinner at our house. Nonetheless, he did, three or four times, when Ray was still seeing him. I attribute his forgetfulness to age.

In a neutral tone, I say, "You didn't come to his funeral."

"Is that a reproach?"

"No, just an observation."

"Ray and I . . ."

He doesn't finish his sentence.

I pour out the tea and say, "I can't believe it was a year ago already."

"Was Marianne there?"

He asks the question with the greatest naturalness.

"Yes, with their children. And their grandchildren."

"So you two got married? Just before?"

I put down the teapot. "Before what?"

"Before it was too late."

"What are you insinuating?"

"Nothing, nothing at all. You're his last wife. Nothing wrong with that. And now you're his . . ." He pauses for a few seconds and then finishes his sentence, enunciating each syllable. ". . . literary executrix."

"I hate that word."

"Which one?"

"'Executrix.'"

"You like the power."

"I'm carrying out his wishes."

"Which you alone seem to know."

I shrug my shoulders. He raises his cup.

His Siouxish features do not relax. He makes no sound as he drinks. Is he really swallowing? He must think I want to poison him.

"You haven't made such a long trip just for that, have you?"

He puts down his cup. "Just for what?"

"For the opportunity to demonstrate your flair for irony."

He lifts his chin as if he were addressing a large gathering. "I've come to clear up a misunderstanding, Joanne. You see, I still have some friends in the profession. Yes, in spite of the ingratitude that characterizes writers, in spite of their vague 'sense of the fundamental decencies'—"

"Douglas, you're not in one of your classes."

"Let me finish, Joanne. Certain things must be said. They must be said here, in this house where Ray's spirit is hovering." (He settles himself comfortably in his armchair.) "My intention is to reveal the person I really am."

"God help us!"

He lets it go. "What else have I done all these years? 'Know me, know the tales I tell.' That's what every one of my stories whispers to its readers."

"*Your* stories?"

"I was the Captain of the Storytellers, if you remember."

I say nothing. I content myself with smiling.

He moves forward in his chair and puts on an afflicted air. "Joanne, please, I'd like you to stop telling anyone who's willing to listen that I 'butchered' his short stories. That's not what I did."

"No, to hear you talk, you only rewrote them."

I'm conscious of the pink patches on his neck.

"Improved them," he says, correcting me.

"What does it matter?"

He sees that I'm going to remain inflexible. A sigh escapes him. I pour myself more tea and say, "I understand you've started a magazine."

"*The Chrysalis.* We have a print run of ten thousand copies."

"For you, that's starting over from scratch."

"Ten thousand," he repeats, as if I've insulted him.

"Great," I say, with a silent prayer for him to leave.

As he doesn't move, I summarize: "So: Your friends have informed you that I'm spreading rumors. You'd like me to put an end to that. And in exchange, you'll stop saying you rewrote Ray's short stories."

"Exactly," he says, scratching his wrist.

"I see things differently."

He looks daggers at me.

"I'm going to republish his stories."

"What?"

"The way they were before the butchery. I'm going to publish them all."

"You're crazy."

"I'm the executrix."

"A disastrous decision—"

"People will judge for themselves. They'll be able to compare the two versions."

"You don't have his versions. There isn't anything left of what he wrote."

"Of course there is. You sold your archives to two universities."

"The manuscripts are illegible. Everything's crossed out in heavy black ink."

"I've hired some experts. They're going to decipher everything."

"You want to destroy my work."

"Your work? Butchering Raymond was your work."

The patches on his skin have turned red. "All right," he says, getting to his feet.

As he remains standing there, I say, without looking at him, "I think we've examined all sides of the question."

He turns and takes a step toward the door. Then he makes

an about-face and says, "Let me raise one point, Joanne. What if the stories from before the 'butchery,' as you call it—what if they turn out to be disappointing? What then?"

I don't say anything. I gaze at him steadily.

"Let's say people read my version and his and compare the two. What if those readers come to the conclusion that I made the stories better, that I transformed them into masterpieces, which they weren't? What if the whole world starts thinking that way? What will be left of Raymond then?"

I remain silent.

"A terrible responsibility, Joanne."

He feels my resolution wavering.

I gather my strength. "I know what I'm doing."

"In that case—"

He opens the door.

"But don't say 'butchery.' Don't say I butchered his stories."

At the instant when the door shuts, I think I hear him say, "I loved him too much to do that to him."

But the wind chimes drown out his words.

JOANNE

The harbor's twenty minutes from here. Nevertheless, I seem to hear its sounds. The seagulls circling the moored freighters. The ropes and cables slapping the masts. And a young woman's voice. She's in a telephone booth in front of the closed bar, trying to get someone to come for her. She can't understand how they could forget her, how they could leave her alone in the harbor, where the lights are going out. She's sobbing, and it wouldn't take much for her to climb into a boat and cross the strait. The next day she'd wake up in the country on the other side.

A new harbor, a new life.

The Drink That Did Him In

"If there's one thing people appreciate about him, it's that nothing goes to his head."

That was the remark you'd hear most often when the subject of the conversation was Max.

His way of laughing for no reason, his schoolboy jokes, and his perennially childlike mug made those who knew him willing to forgive him for anything.

And he had a lot of things to be forgiven for.

His last joke had consisted of dying prematurely, not long after turning fifty.

All we could do was gather and grieve for him, with the dazed, groggy looks of people brought together by the death of a loved one. And yet our faces, sad as they were, sometimes broke into smiles. For nobody was as funny as he was. No one could make us laugh as much as Max.

The funeral had taken place around three o'clock. A buffet was served at our house afterward, and now almost everyone was gone. Only four of us were left on the veranda.

We'd retreated out there so we wouldn't have to clean up right away. Bottles, half-empty glasses, and plates with the remains of food littered the living room. With Fred and me on the veranda were Anne and Victor, our best friends.

A soft summer night was beginning to fall. The chairs we were sitting in, the coffee table and the bottles scattered on it, the empty cage that used to hold my in-laws' nightingale (I'd opened the cage that morning and let the

bird escape)—all the wicker furniture took on a gray hue in
the shade of the veranda.

We hadn't turned on the lamp with the Japanese
lampshade or the strings of lights around the windows. It was
as if we were trying to connect with Max, to communicate
with his spirit, in the darkness.

Max was a writer. Thanks to his books, his spirit would
remain among us. Yes, as long as there were people to read
his work, Max would live on amid the shadows.

I was saying that to myself when Anne came back from
the living room with several bottles. Some of them were
nearly full.

She put down the tray.

"You want to get us drunk," Fred said.

"In homage to Max," I said.

Victor looked at me. He seemed not to understand.

Anne told Fred, "If you two don't drink with Iris and me,
you'll just wind up sorrier."

"We're not so depressed," Victor said.

"A better homage to Max would be not to drink," said
Fred, grabbing a bottle of red wine.

He poured himself some. Victor held out his glass, saying,
"I never saw him drink."

"That's true," Anne said. "Max stopped before I met
you." She turned her attention to a bottle.

Victor looked at me. "He drank like a fish?"

"Let's say he had a lot of fish potential."

That got some loud laughs. It was getting darker and
darker. I couldn't make out Victor's features, but it seemed to

me he wasn't sharing in our hilarity. His tone of voice was curt, staccato.

Victor's an optician. His shop in the center of town is decorated in psychedelic style to attract a young clientele. There's a display of fantasy frames on a tall rack near the door. That sort of thing isn't Victor's cup of tea, but they sell like hotcakes. Anne was the one who came up with the idea.

One of the bottles still held a little Scotch. I gulped down a last swallow of wine and poured the whiskey into my glass.

"Max had so much potential he almost died of it."

"It was ten years ago," Fred said to Victor. "The doctors told him if he didn't stop drinking, he was signing his own death sentence."

"No kidding."

I looked at Anne. I was surprised she'd never told Victor about that.

They've been married for five years. We four and Max had often had dinner together. But Anne had her reasons for not wanting to delve too deeply into the subject of Max.

The two of them had carried on an affair as passionate as it was destructive.

Their excessive consumption of alcohol (they had something like a ménage à trois, with whiskey as the third member of the household) had necessarily led to disaster.

They spent several nights in jail cells. Anne even got her driver's license taken away permanently. She's never told Victor anything. He thinks she doesn't know how to drive.

Although disaster suited Max—as a writer, he made good use of it—Anne began to think about her future. At the age of thirty-nine, she decided to settle down. She left Max and met Victor. Or maybe she met Victor while she was still with Max, nobody knows for sure.

Anne got pregnant pretty quickly. Melody and Lucy, gorgeous twin girls as blond as their mom, will be nine next month. The only times Anne saw Max again after her marriage to Victor were when she came to our house.

Victor finished his glass. Fred offered to refill it. We had enough booze to stay drunk for a week. In the darkness of the veranda, nobody complained.

Anne and Victor were on the sofa. I had the impression they were holding hands. Fred was sitting on the other side of the table. I thought about moving my chair closer to his so I could stroke him, but I spotted a second bottle of Scotch and poured myself another drink instead.

The stridulations of the crickets resounded from the garden. I saw shapes moving in the shrubbery. I listened. Silence fell amid melancholy and drunkenness. I thought we'd just achieved serenity. Was Max's passing filling us with mortal thoughts? Putting the fugitive nature of life in the forefront of our minds? At that moment, death seemed to me no more appalling than the flight of a bird that seizes its chance when you open the door of its cage.

Suddenly Victor bawled out, "He didn't look like it, your Max, but he clung hard to his scrap of existence, right?"

His voice sounded full of bitterness. I looked at Anne. Her body was rigid.

By scooting forward on my chair, I could see they weren't holding hands. Their fists were clenched and their arms pressed tightly against their sides.

I remembered that during the interment, Anne hadn't stayed next to Victor. She'd moved two steps behind him.

He spoke into the silence: "He gnawed on his little life like a bone, didn't he?"

I expected to see Anne shrug her shoulders. Instead she buried her face in her hands.

Fred drawled, "Vic, it's not very charitable to talk about a dead man like that."

Vic had his legs crossed, and he shook his free foot like someone losing patience.

Anne made a clucking sound. "You know he doesn't like to be called 'Vic.'"

Victor said "Max" between his teeth, as though trying to grind up the name.

"Hey, Iris?"

"What?"

"Are you drunk?" Fred asked, searching for my eyes.

"No indeed."

I stood up. Dizziness immediately overcame me. The floor was slipping away under my feet. I held on to my chair.

Then I turned on the lamp. When he saw the light, Fred cried out in relief.

Anne whispered to Victor, "You're really an asshole. He never had anything against you."

"How did he do it?" Victor lashed out in reply. "Why wasn't he jealous of me? Because he had no reason to be, that's why." And he flung his glass onto the coffee table.

His black hair, which had taken a turn for the worse while we were sitting in the dark, was falling to one side of his head.

"No quarreling!" Fred said, reaching to stabilize a bottle he'd knocked off balance.

I steadied it before it could fall to the floor.

Anne had taken off her eyeglasses, a pair with an electric-blue frame that Victor had reluctantly ordered for her. She threw the glasses on the table. "What an asshole you can be! I mean, what an asshole!"

"My name is Victor," he said. His cheeks looked scarlet.

"Did I say 'Vic'?"

"Victor," he repeated, challenging her with his eyes.

I moved past Fred to turn on the lights around the windows. They weren't working. I must have shut off the current with the wall switch.

My legs wobbled. I'm not very big; two glasses of Scotch are enough to give me vertigo. I went back to my chair and sat down.

Fred turned to me. "Darling, would you mind getting us a pitcher of water? With lots of—"

He interrupted himself. He'd just seen the cage. His eyes were half closed. He squinted even more, and his mouth contorted bizarrely.

I thought, *What a stupid mouth my husband has.*

"Where's Gottfried?"

It took me a few seconds to register the name. Then, in an excessively cheerful voice, I said, "I didn't tell you what happened this morning? Gottfried flew off."

"*Flew off?*"

"The bird's name is Gottfried!" Anne said. "That's hilarious."

"I don't find it funny," Victor growled.

He sounded so stuffy I burst out laughing. Anne thought I was laughing with her. "Hilarious . . ." she said.

She slid limply to the pale straw mat that covered the floor. Tears welled up in her eyes.

Fred got to his feet. "Iris, don't tell me you've lost Gottfried."

"It's Max's fault."

"Aha!" said Victor, as if he'd caught him in the act.

"A dead man's fault?"

"Frigging Max!" Anne whispered.

The effluvia of alcohol invaded the veranda. They made the air sticky. I suppose I was as red as Fred and Victor.

Only Anne, who was keeping her eyes fixed on the floor, looked pale. From time to time, mocking spasms shook her body. "Gottfried, where are you?" she trilled between hiccups.

Fred was waiting for my answer.

"I thought about Max all morning."

"What does that have to do with Gottfried?" Fred asked, his eyes flashing.

Anne squealed, "Gottfried!"

"Let her explain herself," Victor said, as if we were in the midst of an interrogation.

"Look at this," Anne said indignantly. "The men are ganging up on the women!"

"That has nothing to do with it," Victor grumbled.

The glass Anne was bringing to her lips muffled her reply, which was "Shut up, Vic. Don't let 'em push you around, Iris!"

Fred was still glaring at me.

"When I opened the cage to feed Gottfried, he was standing on his trapeze, stiff as a board. So stiff I wondered if he might be dead. I tapped on the cage, I flicked it—"

" 'Flicked it'?" Fred repeated, round-eyed.

"Dumb broads . . ."

"Don't let 'em push you around, Iree."

"I gave the bars a few taps to wake him up."

"But he wasn't sleeping! Gottfried never sleeps!"

"Gottfried was biding his time," Victor said.

"In any case, he didn't budge. At all. I thought maybe he'd wake up for food. I went back to the front of the cage, opened it, and picked up the bowl of birdseed. Then I shook the bowl through the open door."

"*The open door!*"

"I must have been thinking about Max. Yes. That was it. I was remembering his poem about a nightingale. Or maybe a robin, I can't remember. Anyway, just at that moment, Gottfried flew out and disappeared."

"He has to be somewhere! He has to be somewhere nearby!"

Fred started turning round and round, as if the bird had just escaped.

"Come back, Free-dee!" Anne screamed at the top of her voice.

"You'll never see him again," Victor opined.

"My mother's nightingale!" Fred was searching everywhere on the veranda.

Beyond the sofa where Victor sat, sipping his wine at brief, regular intervals, the garden was breathing the night.

That morning, without hesitating an instant, the

nightingale had leaped into the greenery. He hadn't let himself be distracted by seeds.

I put my hand on Fred's shoulder. I said, "It's not so serious, my love."

"Spoken like a dumb broad," Victor said.

I shot a look at him. He smoothed his hair with his free hand and kept his eyes away from mine. With his other hand, he was shaking his glass and splashing drops of wine on his yellow shirt. *A yellow shirt for Max's funeral*, I thought.

Fred's moaning was beginning to exasperate me. "That's enough, Fred," I told him. "Your mouth is stupid."

"*What?*"

"I'm sure she did it on purpose, that stuff with the bird. Yeah. I think she wanted to let it go back to nature."

Anne struck Victor on the knee. He smiled broadly.

His words had inflamed Fred. He came close and jumped down my throat.

"You never had any respect for my mother! And now that she's dead, you . . . you want to get rid of her things. You want to liquidate Mom."

Hilda, Fred's mother, had died in April. He wasn't getting over it. As for me, I'd never felt much affection for her, a bitter woman who'd fire off barrages of reproaches with a satisfied smile on her face.

"Nice little trick," Fred said, drinking straight out of the bottle. "With Max as your accomplice. Doesn't surprise me."

"I thought you were friends."

"Max was my friend. But he was also a first-class son of a bitch."

"Well said!"

Anne hit Victor again. This time he grabbed her wrist. They started to wrestle.

Fred went on, sounding groggy: "Who was proud to have him for a friend? A writer who put us in his stories, big deal. Proud he was mocking us, is that it?"

"He never mocked you."

"Come on," said Fred, no longer thinking about Gottfried. "I'm not the deceived husband in 'Guess Who's Coming to See Us'?"

"But no, it's . . ."

I left my sentence in suspense.

The deceived husband in Max's story was Victor. Max wrote it to avenge himself on Anne, who had just left him. But feature for feature, the husband in the story *looked* like Fred.

"Exactly," said Victor, rising to his feet. "I have the honor to inform you that the deceived husband in 'Guess Who's Coming to See Us' is me."

He sketched an arabesque with his glass. Then he brought it to his mouth and drained it.

Anne was staring into space. I was surprised to see her get up, very slowly, spreading out her arms. Her open palms moved farther and farther away from each other, like she was preparing to catch a ball that kept getting bigger.

"Anne, what are you doing?"

She didn't answer me. She was still staring into space. Then she clapped her hands and cried, "Missed it!"

I realized she was hunting a mosquito. Without any transition, she sat back down, turned to Victor, and said, "I didn't know you read his stories."

"Why wouldn't I? They're in our library."

He said that in a neutral voice, taking us as his witnesses, Fred and me.

"*My* library. You don't read anything but golf magazines."

"Well, the items under discussion are in our living room."

"Max's books?" Fred asked, jeering.

I gave him a reproachful look. Why was he throwing oil on the fire?

"Wait, wait. It's too funny. Victor, who never reads books, has devoured all of Max's."

"Fred, that's enough."

Victor explained: "I'm interested in literature that talks about my wife."

"I'm not in 'Guess Who's Coming to See Us,'" Anne declared. "The character you're thinking of is Iris."

"That's what I thought too," Fred observed. "The girl dresses like Iris. With her high boots and her Bakelite bracelets."

"Don't be fooled, that's a decoy," Victor said. "The slut in 'Guess Who's Coming'—"

"I can't believe it," I interrupted him. "We're fighting over who's in one of Max's stories!"

"He was obliged to put us in," Victor said. "He had no imagination."

"He used us," Fred said, going him one better.

"Oh, go on. You're ridiculous, both of you."

"It's pure jealousy," Anne said. "You would both have

loved to have Max's talent. He immersed himself in his friends."

"He immersed himself in his friends but most of all in his booze."

"I thought we were here to pay tribute to him."

"*You're* here to pay tribute to him. If it was up to me—"

"Fine," Anne said. "Let's get this settled once and for all."

"Why would I pay tribute to a guy who banged my wife?" said Fred, sniffing the bottom of his glass.

"I *never*—"

"I'm sick of this," Anne said, getting up again.

Victor grabbed her. "You're not going anywhere!"

Anne's foot struck the coffee table, knocking over glasses and bottles. This time I didn't react. I just watched them all fall.

Fred laughed ferociously.

"Victor, you're completely loaded," Anne said, freeing herself from him.

She massaged her wrist and stared blackly at Victor. He shouted, "You're not leaving before you say who the twins' father is!"

We all froze.

Victor pointed a finger at Anne. With her lids half shut and her eyes brightened by drink, she withstood her husband's stare.

"Now," he added.

I observed Anne. A smile flitted across her lips. I knew her fondness for provocation. Under the influence of alcohol, that tendency could turn into perversity.

I looked at Fred, silently urging him to calm the other two down. But he was finding their quarrel delightful.

"The twins . . ." Victor said. "Are they mine? Or someone else's?"

There was no bitterness in his voice. He simply wanted to know. To clear up a doubt.

Wine dripped from the wicker table onto the straw mat.

Speaking softly, Anne said, "What makes you think—"

"Their eyes."

"This is all because they didn't get your eyes?"

"Melody's and Lucy's eyes are blue around the pupil and gray around the outer edge."

"They have my mother's eyes. As you well know."

"Max's eyes were like that."

"No, they weren't."

"What do you mean they weren't?"

"You should know, you made his glasses for him. Max's eyes were gray around the iris."

Victor frowned.

"Look at his pictures on the backs of his books."

"They're in black and white."

"For heaven's sake, Victor! Then get a paternity test."

"I'd rather believe you."

"You can."

He picked up the only glass that was still standing and emptied it in one gulp. "Good," he said.

We all breathed sighs of relief.

That could have turned out bad. I'd just realized that Anne hadn't denied having a relationship with Max after her marriage. Victor had understood. Or maybe Max's story had made him understand before this.

All of a sudden I got angry at Max. It was just like him to cause a lot of trouble.

"He couldn't get it up," Anne said.

"What?"

"He was too drunk. I reminded him of that fact when he claimed to be the girls' father. But he had too much pride."

Anne shook her head, as if she missed Max in spite of all his faults. Fred let out an incredulous laugh. I was petrified.

Without taking his eyes off Anne, Victor nodded. His nostrils flared. You would have thought he was breathing in the alcoholic vapors. "All the better," he said.

Anne looked at us, at Fred and me, as if she was challenging us to say a single word.

"All the better," Victor repeated, although no one knew what he was alluding to.

His head was tilted to one side. For the space of an instant, I feared he was going to go all wobbly. He seemed to have no idea where he was.

He crinkled his eyes. Had he just figured out the meaning of his wife's words?

At that point, I said, "Have you all seen how much booze we've put away? I mean, have you got any idea?"

There was some tittering. Anne uttered a moan, but whether it was joyful or appalled I couldn't tell.

"Say now," Fred remarked, surveying the disaster.

Victor wasn't with us anymore. His brain was on fire. It frightened me to think he might sober up completely.

Anne had stopped paying attention to him. She said, "We're about to drink ourselves to death!"

"Soon we'll be joining Max!" Fred shouted.

"Except the drink that did Max in wasn't wine or whiskey . . ."

They all shut up.

"Not wine or whiskey," I said again. "The drink that did him in was water."

They remained dumbfounded.

"It's never occurred to any of you? Max starts drinking when he's fifteen. The first time is when he goes fishing and takes along a thermos full of whiskey. He hides his drinking from his parents. He hides his drinking from his friends. And he hides his drinking from the doctors in the hospitals he winds up in. For thirty-five years, he drinks. And when the miracle takes place, when he quits alcohol and starts drinking water, what happens? He dies."

"Holy shit," someone whispered.

They all burst out laughing.

Fred elaborated my point, talking over the laughter: "He drinks like a fish and then when he switches to water, he croaks. He kicks the bucket."

An orgasmic howl escaped Anne.

Fred was holding his sides. My laughter mingled with theirs.

"He kicks the bucket!" Victor exclaimed fiercely. He repeated the words several times, as if taking revenge.

We all had tears in our eyes. I don't know how long our giggling fit lasted. Eventually the laughter died down and everything grew calm again.

We could hear crickets. A cloud of insects was dancing around the lampshade. It was time to go back into the living room. Time to leave the veranda, whose atmosphere affected us so strangely.

Anne gathered up the bottles while I collected the glasses. After a few seconds, there wasn't so much as a square inch of free space on the tray.

Walking into the living room, Fred and Victor started chatting again. What was surprising was that they were chatting about Max, and casually at that. "So I take it he was an alcoholic?" Victor asked. "I knew he was the anxious type, but I didn't think—"

"Alcoholic *and* anxious. He was afraid of going blind. An absurd fear."

"Totally unfounded."

"You examined his eyes, you should know."

As they spoke, they moved apart.

Anne smiled. As if she remembered something she couldn't reveal.

More of their conversation reached us from the living room.

"Max was blind when it came to the essential things in his life. But he was in no danger of losing his sight."

"I'm terribly sorry," Anne said in a low voice.

"I'll be able to get it out. I've got a lot of products that work on this mat."

"No, I mean . . ." She looked at me. Tears different from those we'd just been shedding filled her eyes. She carried the bottles away, saying, "I'm going to fix us something to eat."

In the living room, Fred and Victor lit up cigars.

I looked around. It had been optimistic of me to say I'd get the wine stain out. The paper towels hadn't done a very thorough job.

Even though it wasn't cold, I felt a shiver run over me.

I didn't feel like going back inside. Nobody was calling me; I could stay out on the veranda for a while. I switched off the lamp and tried the window lights again. They worked. Then, lured on by the fragrant evening air, I took a little walk in the garden.

The trees were shivering too. Creatures shifted about, moving in the branches and the night.

I thought again about Max. I wondered if he would have liked my little disquisition on the drink that did him in. How would he have told that story? More cruelly, no doubt.

Frigging Max. Who'll immerse himself in us now?

I moved away from the veranda to a part of the lawn the window lights didn't quite reach.

That was when I saw him.

Gottfried. A yard away from me, hopping in the grass. I froze. He got closer to the light. Was he looking for his cage? Did he want to return to his prison?

I heard Fred's voice, then Anne's, calling me inside the house. "Iris? Iris?"

I leaned down to the bird. "Go on," I said. "Go away, Gottfried. Don't go back to your cage." He hopped to one side, skirting the porch.

"You're free now."

He entered the shadows. I couldn't see him anymore. I hesitated, waited.

Then I went back to the house and rejoined the others.

SELECTED BIBLIOGRAPHY

Adelman, Bob, and Raymond Carver. *Carver Country: The World of Raymond Carver*. Scribner, 1990.

Carver, Maryann Burk. *What It Used to Be Like: A Portrait of My Marriage to Raymond Carver*. St. Martin's Press, 2006.

Carver, Raymond. *Collected Stories*. Edited by William Stull and Maureen Carroll. Library of America, 2009.

Gallagher, Tess. *Deux audacieux. Auprès de Raymond Carver*. Arléa, 2001.

Halpert, Sam. *Raymond Carver: An Oral Biography*. University of Iowa Press, 1995.

Lish, Gordon, ed. *All Our Secrets Are the Same: New Fiction from Esquire*. Esquire, 1976.

————. *The Secret Life of Our Times: New Fiction from Esquire*. Doubleday, 1973.

Romon, Philippe. *Parlez-moi de Carver*. Agnès Viénot, 2003.

Sklenicka, Carol. *Raymond Carver: A Writer's Life*. Scribner, 2009.

ACKNOWLEDGMENTS

In the course of his work on this book, the author benefited from a writer's residence in the Villa Marguerite Yourcenar and from a grant given by the Conseil Général du Nord. He thanks Achmy Halley and his team for their warm welcome.

The author likewise thanks John Baule, Tom Chiarella, Marion Coutarel, Hervé Delouche, Jeanne Guyon, Karen and Henner Krueger, Aurélien Masson, Nathaniel Rich, Rebecca Saletan, Elisabeth Samama, Lilas Seewald, and Robert Stewart.

Printed in the United States
by Baker & Taylor Publisher Services